PARADIGM SHIFT

A REVERBERATION OF BLOODSHED AND TEARS.

Prateek Singh

INDIA • SINGAPORE • MALAYSIA

ISBN 979-8-88749-304-6

Paradigm Shift

Change is a natural law and is imminent.
If you resist change, you resist life.

Acknowledgement

Having an idea for a book and converting the idea into a book are two entirely different things. It is hard to find a connection between the events that don't have many similarities.

Thank you! Akanksha Sinha for suggesting the title and listening to the idea.

My friend Kumar Abhishek for being an observer and helping improve my storytelling and for his Legal advice. Thanks.

My family always stood by my side and never discouraged me in this journey. I thank you for your support.

I like to thank the various news reporters from around the world and The articles published on Wikipedia, the New York Times and Al-Jazeera for covering so many updates about the global geopolitics events that helped me form the very basis of this story.

Finally, my Publishing Manager Mr Barath Raj Muthukumar, Thank you for being extremely patient during the whole journey and the entire team of Notion press for making publishing easy for many upcoming authors. I would like to wish them all the very best in their future endeavours.

I pray for all the people who have lost their lives in war.

This book is just a small tribute to all of them.

Contents

1. Underground 9

2. The Massacre..19

3. The Family Affair...30

4. The Broken Man..43

5. Rebuilding from Scratch....................................52

6. Manhattan Life 65

7. Paying the Dues 76

8. The Misguided Youth.......................................85

9. The Cyber Warfare..98

10. The New York Attack..111

11. The Civil War...117

12. Revelations 136

13. Dead End 149

14. The Evil Game-plan 162

15. Terms of Reality 172

Chapter 1

Underground

(February 2010, Dimona, Israel.)

In a remote area of the Negev desert, lies a radar facility with towers approximately 200 meters in height, which can track anything down. It can track a missile launched from southern Russia and keep tabs on aerial movements even in Iraq—such is the enormous power of the Israeli radar station, which the United States of America now controls. For the first time in history, the United States has established a proper military research facility located beyond American soil. The facility is situated on the outskirts of Dimona, in a completely deserted wasteland in the Negev desert. Just when you think there is nothing around you amidst the empty stretches of dunes, out of nowhere, in the middle of the desert, you can spot the high towers of Israel surrounded by circular lights—as if they were designed for an alien spaceship's landing pad. The facility comprises no permanent structure—just two small rooms. However, more than 60 US personnel live underground in this highly radioactive zone.

Under the ground, there is a highly advanced facility with high-tech technologies that even the Israelis are not allowed to glimpse. The facility uses modern stealth technologies so that no satellite in the sky can penetrate its walls. Russia was not happy with the gesture that the Israelis showed and warned them of the consequences shortly. The staff mainly comprises technicians, scientists, and US armed forces personnel. There is a specific need for armed soldiers in the facility. They have to protect the team of highly qualified, skilled analysts and scientists as they gather very sensitive intel from the skies of Israel. The structure consists of modern radar monitoring stations, data storage rooms, control rooms to analyze everything, and a temporary quarter that has been set up for its staff.

A convoy of US military vehicles was headed for Dimona from Jerusalem. The convoy carried the newly-armed soldier to a top-secret radar station. Private Daniel Ryan was the newest army member sent to Dimona to protect its crucial staff members. As the other soldiers talked about their upcoming destination, he seemed lost in his world. As the convoy reached its destination, all the soldiers were escorted by the upper ground staff, including a handful of soldiers who waited outside a small room—the only visible structure from the outside. Their job was to guide the newcomers to the underground station.

The platoon started descending a staircase 100 feet below the ground. There were at least 15 recruits from various branches of the US military. Many of the soldiers were thrilled about this unique experience that was about to happen, except for Daniel, who seemed to be disinterested in the job. Daniel was from the US Marine Corps. He was of medium stature, not more than five feet seven inches in height, with big eyes and a round face.

The overall look on his face was taut—as if he was in some deep-rooted pain. His body language was very sluggish and dull. However, he looked more experienced than the other soldiers who arrived with him. He held the rank of a *Private* that did not match his age. All of them were instructed to wait for the head of the facility to come and give them further instructions. As they arrived, older platoons were on their way to their respective bases. The guys who left were far more relieved than those who had just come. The newcomers did not understand this sign. A few soldiers started discussing, "What the hell is this place?"

One answered, "I don't know, man. It looks like a science lab!"

The soldiers were pleased and thrilled a moment ago. A question stuck in all their minds—*why do the soldiers, who are leaving, look so happy and relieved?* This question made their excited faces lose their luster. The feeling of enthusiasm was gone. However, Daniel had no such expression on his face or any thought in his mind. He was impassive and deeply involved in his thoughts.

The director of the facility was awaited. The lift opened, and an old lady stepped out from behind the door with two of her staff members. She was an older woman in her late 60s, though her body language reflected immense experience. She was of a relatively shorter height with short blonde hair. The wrinkles on her face suggested that she was just an ordinary old lady, but her position suggested that she yielded power. She started walking casually and came close to the soldiers. She began addressing the new soldiers by saying, "I'm Diana! As long as you do what you are told, there will be nothing to worry about. Welcome to Dimona, or rather, I should say, beneath the Negev."

She started moving toward the control room. Her staff guided the soldiers to their respective quarters—it was a very brief orientation.

Daniel entered his chamber. It was not a chamber. The room felt like it was designed for prisoners by its appearance, but it had been upgraded to look like the staff's personal quarters. It just had a door. Windows were out of the question, but the air circulated from above to below through a ventilation shaft. He knew by its look that the room was not a place for him to live for a long time. After staring at the space and its solid walls for a few more minutes, he thought that it was a prison cell. There was nowhere to go except upstairs. He could not go outside. This feeling was enough to make him understand that this particular journey was not going to be as smooth as his past deployments. He put his belongings down, took out a picture from his bag, and hung the photo of his old squad on the wall. Suddenly, he was taken aback, just by looking at the picture. The picture had six members of the Marine squad. From the environment in the background, it could be noticed that it was some desert—maybe from Afghanistan or Iraq. Above the team, there was a marking with bold red ink which stated, ***Death before Dishonor***. He then lay down restlessly and went off to sleep.

In the next few days, he realized that there was nothing significant about that job, as there was nothing substantial for a marine person who was stationed at an underground facility. He had to stand guard in the control room with a few more soldiers. The authority running the facility wanted the soldiers to act like puppets as there was no intrusion—Israel was already protecting it. Daniel walked toward the control room wearing his marine uniform, thinking that he had to pass this phase of his life. The only thing that comforted him was that this posting would not last for more than a few months.

Daniel remembered an incident from his past. In 2005, Staff Sargent Daniel Ryan was posted in Iraq for more than six months. Before his deployment, the US began its invasion of Iraq in early 2003 due to the dictatorship of Saddam Hussein, the President of Iraq at that time. As per many conspiracy theories, the Hussein regime possessed chemical weapons—a threat to the US government. Some experts claimed that the US had always been pursuing their oil and natural resources. On the edge of Saddam Hussein's image as a tyrant, the United States conducted horrifying atrocities, and the world just watched in silence.

Daniel was a decorated soldier, earning many medals in his military career. He was an experienced soldier and a true patriot—ready to sacrifice his life at any moment. Sometimes, these soldiers carry out the most horrendous crimes in the name of patriotism. Staff Sergeant Daniel underwent such a case. War is a very complex mechanism in itself—it is not easy to understand it through the eyes and expressions of civilians. Daniel was in the US Marines' third battalion of the First Regiment. The task assigned to the Marines was to carry out raids and protect their units against the insurgent forces of Iraq. Daniel was ready for this second tour of his duty in Iraq. He had already served in Afghanistan before.

He met his fellow Marines who had gathered from different parts of the US. The soldiers had to perform daily military drills to counter the enemy forces, including close-quarter combat and highly-intense physical activities, which were designed to not only exhaust the soldiers but also to make them strong and ready to face adverse conditions in real-life combat situations. Daniel was well regarded in his unit due to his past successful missions in Afghanistan. He soon became popular and was taken very seriously by his juniors and the senior members of his command.

(Dimona, Israel, 2010).

He disliked the job immensely and never really tried interacting with others. The job was not designed for a soldier—it was more of a punishment. His body language was enough to make clear the agony that he was going through at that time. The facility also had tremendous radiation, which was odd for a radar facility, but there were warning signs everywhere. A group of personnel sitting inside the control room doing their regular shift started a conversation about Saddam Hussein and the US invasion of Iraq. The war began in 2003 and lasted almost a decade until it was over in 2013. The conversation made Daniel, who was standing in the corner, a little uncomfortable and he began to move toward his room. It triggered something in his mind. As soon as he sat down, he lit a cigarette. He got restless and worried. He wanted to get out of that place and be with his family. In the next few days, he gradually started consuming alcohol and started getting very tense while remembering something. He used to stare at the only picture of his squad, which was hung on the wall. That particular picture reminded him daily what he did back in Iraq. He mourned something that had happened a long time ago. External wounds heal with time, but internal wounds do not heal quickly. These wounds are like drinking small portions of poison that gradually start killing you slowly and painfully.

A few days passed. Daniel woke up suddenly in the morning with some flashbacks from his past war in his thoughts. He was sweating. This was becoming like a nightmare for him, and he realized that it was just a dream and went to freshen up. The feeling of guilt was written on his face, but he could not express it himself. He thought that he did not deserve to be a soldier. He felt as though he had disappointed everyone. He did not want to hold a gun despite being a soldier. He walked toward the facility and sat at a desk with the same look of uneasiness.

Meanwhile, the facility's staff noticed Daniel's behavior, and Diana was well informed of his situation. She knew something was wrong with the lad and the willingness to know the reason behind his discomfort made Diana feel curious. Diana began to observe Daniel from the control room. However, Daniel seemed uninterested in engaging in any conversation. He looked at her and tried to maintain distance—allowing neither her nor anyone else a chance to interact with him. He smoked cigarettes and avoided talking to anyone. This was his regular daily routine. The feeling of guilt and shame started manifesting in his sleep as nightmares.

Daniel always had the same nightmare in which he saw himself in an incident where the Marines were in so much distress, shock, and fear after an IED (improvised explosive device) exploded and disrupted their convoy. At least five dead bodies were lying near a stationed car. It looked like they were shot from a close distance. The IED had exploded, but it did not kill any Iraqis. A marine was killed and two of them were injured. Daniel looked like he was ready to execute anyone who dared to come his way. He looked at the fellow marine lying on the street, torn apart in half by the intense explosion. The Marines shot many Iraqis in retaliation as a result of the explosion. Daniel ensured that this incident was not narrated similarly. He imposed his version of the story on his fellow Marines. Daniel and his company moved forward after listening to the gunfire. They were moving toward the crowded allies with the explicit intention of killing them. He saw his unit open fire at an unarmed civilian, killing everyone who came into sight. He was merely observing the incident. He saw a little girl, lying injured in a corner. Her face was damaged and she was unconscious. His fellow Marines started checking whether everybody was dead by putting a bullet to their heads. As soon as one of the Marines came close to finishing off the little girl, Daniel stopped him by saying, "She is dead," even though she was not dead. Daniel saw his company rejoicing over their triumphant victory over the innocent people. He even saw his one his fellow marines urinate over a dead Iraqi's head. Daniel did not do anything to stop that misbehavior. The girl's damaged face haunted him each day. He woke up restlessly and in tears. That became a daily habit for him. After waking up, he also remembered talking to his fellow Marines in a post-combat incident and briefing his subordinates, "They were trying to run. That's when the IED exploded and killed these men, Clear!" he said commandingly.

Daniel's situation was getting worse with each passing day. The indulgences in alcohol and cigarettes started deteriorating his health, which could not be ignored any further. Diana was informed of his health's current situation. She asked her staff to bring him to a medical facility for his treatment as soon as possible. Daniel started having anxiety attacks, which became unbearable. He was taken to the medical facility and his treatment began. The doctors did not find anything significant—just alcoholism that created high blood pressure and anxiety. He was soon discharged from the medical facility underground. As soon as he felt good enough, he rushed to the command center room, grabbed a satellite phone, and called his wife, Linda. He felt relaxed just after listening to her voice. After months, she was glad to hear her husband's voice and asked, "Where have you been, Dan?"

Daniel replied, "Israel. I can only tell you this much. How are the children doing?"

"They miss you for sure. Listen, I heard about the court-martial thing. Is that true?"

Daniel took a deep breath, and after a moment's pause, he said, "Yes, it is true—just don't let the children know now."

Daniel could hear the sound of sobbing from the other side of the line. He said, "Don't worry, Linda, I will not let us down. There will be another way."

Linda said, "Just come back home. We need you to be here, not there."

Daniel replied, gathering his strength, "Yes, Linda. I'm coming home in just a few more days. Love you. Bye."

He kept the phone down. His hands were shivering, and tears of sorrow rolled down from his eyes. He wanted to leave that place so badly.

He could not wait any longer. He was desperate to talk to someone badly. He never thought Diana could be his sole refuge in this mess. He remembered an incident in which the Gulf and international media highly contradicted his version of the story.

Witnesses claimed that the Marines went inside the houses and killed everyone who came into their sight, including women and children. An Iraqi journalist named Tanaz was intensely monitoring every step of the incident. She presented evidence that was very hard to evade. After close inspection, she made progress in her research and showed facts such that the US Military had to release a statement on her account. The only serving victim of the massacre, the little girl whom Daniel used to see in his dreams, narrated the whole incident in order. The US Military department summoned Daniel. He recorded his statement and stuck with the same version that he had decided on a year ago.

However, after investigating, Colonel Navaro said, "Staff Sergeant Daniel Ryan, I have evidence that says otherwise. Do you still want to stick to your story? Otherwise, there is an option—you can tell me what happened there."

Daniel did not say a word—how could he? He had to hide the truth. He remained quiet for an apparent reason. He thought of his family and said, "Sir, I'm telling you the truth," after taking a deep, deep breath.

He was lying but could not get to terms with reality. Colonel showed him pictures of the incident where he was seen standing near the dead bodies of people who did not die due to the IED. Daniel was shocked and did not know what to say any further. "You will tell me the truth, and until you do so, you are not serving us. Dismissed." Daniel saluted the Colonel and went out of the chamber. Daniel knew that he would not be able to hide the truth forever.

Later that night, he was watching television with his family. Then Colonel Navaro released a statement testifying that the IED did not kill the fifteen Iraqi civilians who had died in Haditha. That was enough for the media to think that a war crime had been committed and they were after the names of the culprit.

Daniel suddenly froze after listening to that statement. He knew he was guilty but was not ready to face it. He knew he could not run from it forever. He had to take the first step.

Linda said, "Come on, children, time for bed, go on."

Daniel's daughters, Jessica, who was 12 years old, and Elizabeth, who was just six years old, were too young to understand these complex situations. They were instructed to go to bed immediately by their mother. As soon as they left for bed, Linda asked, "What happened there? Can you tell me the truth? I'm your wife, God damn it! I should know what you did there."

Daniel lied again and said, "I already told you the truth, Linda. They are trying to frame me."

"I hope you are telling me the truth, Dan. Just tell me the truth while you still can," said Linda.

"But I have told you that we didn't kill anyone. It was the bomb which did," replied Daniel, feeling scared.

Daniel heard his cell phone ring. It was Linda's father who wanted an answer as well. Mr. William asked, "Son, what is this going on with Navarro?"

"They're all lies. Don't listen to them. They are trying to frame me," said Daniel.

"Don't worry, Son. I will help you out with this," said William reassuringly.

Mr. William told the associated press, "Daniel could never do such a cowardly act. He is a true patriot—a decorated Marine and a proud American."

Linda also tried to save her husband from that allegation game by posting articles on her blog. However, that did not help. But they had to try as they were his family.

(Back to Dimona.)

Daniel then walked straight toward the Chief's office. As soon as he had reached the office, he knocked on her door. Her name was boldly engraved as **Diana Francis**. Just as he entered, he saw Diana sitting comfortably on her chair. Daniel said, "Ma'am, I want to speak to you privately."

Diana said, "You are not allowed to use our communication network for a personal chat."

Daniel was slightly frightened and said, "I had to make that call—it was an emergency." "Hmm! Is there something you want to tell me, Soldier?"

Daniel looked at Diana but could not gather the courage to tell her anything. He remained quiet, and after a minute Diana uttered, *Haditha.* Does it sound familiar to you, Soldier?"

Daniel's expression changed and he could not look at her face anymore. He looked down as if the judge had confronted him for his crime and declared him guilty. As he remained silent, Diana said again, "Haditha, Iraq, 2005! Do you remember anything now?"

Daniel became agitated and said, "Stop playing this game. You don't know anything about me."

"Well, I do, Staff Sergeant Daniel Ryan. I guess I do."

Daniel was astonished and thought to himself, *how did she know that I used to hold the rank of Staff Sergeant before the demotion?* He figured that it was not worth messing with a lady like her. He replied politely, "Ma'am, you don't know what happened there."

"I don't—you will enlighten me."

"But how do you know everything about me?" asked Daniel politely.

"We are having this conversation underground—where only demons dwell, not humans. This place is one the most critical secrets kept out of human reach, so don't talk about secrets to me in this place."

Daniel knew it was about time that he had to reveal everything to her.

Chapter 2

The Massacre

Daniel started narrating the whole incident to Diana.

It was the 19th of November 2005, in Hadith, Iraq. The insurgent forces compelled the Marines to open fire many times by then. Local intelligence suggested that many Iraqi local people did not support collation forces. It was becoming difficult to choose between the local citizens and insurgent groups daily. Haditha soon became a place of conflict due to the Haditha Dam—the hydroelectric power plant. Daniel was sitting in the quarter after some drill exercises. After the intense session, four more Marines were exhausted post-workout in the Marine resting quarter.

Farrell, Hill, and Hunter were discussing the situation. Dan said, "Something is wrong with the locals, man! They are confused, and they aren't sure which side to choose."

Farrell agreed with Dan, but Hill said, "We brought ourselves here and created a mess in this country."

Hunter disagreed and said, "Are you trying to say that Hussein's regime was good enough for Iraq?"

Hill replied, "No, but who are we to intervene in another country's problems? First Afghanistan and now Iraq, and who knows how many more are yet to come?"

Hunter responded, "Are you a soldier or a coward, man? You shouldn't have joined the Marine."

"I lost someone very close in Afghanistan," said Hill.

Captain Shepherd listened to everything but did not participate in the conversation till then. Standing outside the door, he suddenly smashed the door down. He roared, "Everyone loses someone or something. It's war! God damn it! Not some TV reality show!"

All of the Marines got up in a hurry and got frightened. He tried to instruct and force them not to be faint of heart. He believed that they should fight and die or quit and go home. He added, "We follow orders, not emotions, understood?"

As he came closer, "Hill, are we clear, you coward? You know you can still quit and leave now. I won't let you put some illusionary fairy tale ideas into my soldiers' heads. We are here to fight other people's wars, which they couldn't fight themselves. Are we clear here?"

Hill nodded and said, "Affirmative, Sir."

The local insurgents knew that the Marines followed a specific route. They were planning to hit them soon. The insurgent was not as equipped as the US Marines, so they had to rely upon AK-47 assault rifles and IEDs, which were very reliable for these militias' groups. An IED is usually filled with explosives in a propane tank. A cell phone is attached to the portable bomb, thus acting as a trigger mechanism. Due to its portability, it can be transported easily, without getting noticed. The locals' funded terrorist groups were termed insurgents by the Marines' forces. The locals backed up these groups. They could camouflage while passing through the towns without getting caught. The group's local leader in the Haditha area was conducting a highly secret meeting outside the city and had gathered his henchmen as well as assembled a new IED device.

The leader asked, "Who all are ready to take revenge for your brothers and sisters?"

Two men volunteered by raising their hands.

"*Masha Allah!*" the leader said, "Brothers, are you ready for true *Jihad*?"

"Yes, brother," said the two men.

The leader demonstrated how one had to plant and trigger the IED device. He also gave them vital intel about the marine route. He asked, "Are you ready?" Can you do this for your country?"

"Yes, we are ready. It is about time that they need to learn a lesson and step away from our nation. *Allah hu Akbar!*" all of them repeated.

They also carried AK-47 rifles—a very important symbol for these fighters. Their only concern was the check post, which they could not deviate from, but their minds were entirely determined and focused only on their target. They hired a local truck, which was transporting vegetables to Haditha City. They acted as though they were local farmers and merchants.

They had an adrenaline rush as they reached the check post while carrying an IED, although they were ready to die. A soldier started checking them after calling them to step out. They cooperated. However, the truck was not checked thoroughly and they were allowed to enter the city. One of the insurgents said, "Brother, Allah is with us on this mission."

"Keep quiet," said the mature one, addressing the young lad who was enthusiastic about the task.

They carried the rifles and the disarmed IED bags as they approached the town of Haditha. They searched for the spot that was ideal for placing and triggering the IED. Reece was done and they started digging a pothole at the corner of the road to place the IED. They continued their work for a few hours, and after the bomb's placement, they spotted a perfect place from where they could monitor the event. They kept in mind the range from where the mobile signal was optimal. They found a house and knocked on the front door. As soon as the door opened, they rushed in deliberately and forcefully, making the family panic. The family was unable to resist as they were carrying guns. They told them to remain calm and promised that nobody would be harmed. They moved upstairs. The family had to cooperate. They reached the rooftop and checked the signal on their mobile phones. They viewed the site through binoculars. Everything was set—now, all they had to do was wait.

The following day, the third battalion and the first Marines were on their way to resupply the convoy from Baghdad to Haditha. Michael Jameson, Josh Hill, Hunter Evans, and Samuel Farrell led the convoy in a Humvee. The next Humvee carried Staff Sergeant Daniel Ryan, Captain Joseph Shepard, and two more Marines. That Humvee was a security vehicle. Shepherd was angry for some reason. He hated the Iraqi people because he believed that the Iraqi people deserved someone like Saddam Hussein only. Daniel did not like his idea entirely but he appreciated his way of thinking. Josh, who was driving the lead Humvee, said, "Look at this place. It is an empty stretch of barren wasteland."

Jameson said, "I need some more sleep, man."

Hill, as usual, was sad due to his past in which he had lost his elder brother and Hunter was in the mood for a conversation. The rock music was playing and Hunter was head-banging to the tune. He said, "Come on, baby! Yeah," and was trying to involve them in the music.

They reached Haditha and were on their way to their camp. They did not know what was waiting for them.

The insurgent was on high alert. They had spotted the Humvees from a distance. "Get ready," one of the guys screamed.

As soon as the convoy reached the spot, they called the number. It triggered the cell phone and the IED blasted so fiercely that it tore apart the iron vehicle into two pieces. Everyone in the other truck was shocked by the immense noise and the explosion created by the bomb. Daniel screamed, "IED! Get off the truck now, damn it!"

Shepard and the rest of the Marines quickly took position outside, "Watch for insurgents. Scan for targets. Eyes on the houses," said Daniel.

Daniel quickly reached his mates. He saw Josh Hill lying in two pieces and rushed toward him. The impact of the blast had killed him instantly. Jameson survived but remained unconscious. "Evans. Farrell!" screamed Daniel, "Can you both stand?"

"Yes! Dan, yes."

Shepard spotted a car near the blast site, pointed a gun, and screamed, "Step out now!"

While the insurgents rejoiced in their victory, they quickly came out of the house and ran toward the other side of the street. They open-fired randomly without any target. Daniel alerted his fellow Marines to get ready. Daniel, now engulfed in rage and seeing Hill's body, yelled at the Iraqis who were standing next to their car in a surrendering pose and facing the opposite side, "You morons think you can kill us? Do you think you can mess with us? Where are the shooters? Tell me now!"

The innocent Iraqis could not understand anything as they did not know English. One of the Marines translated Dan's words, but they did not know anything. They remained quiet. Out of sheer rage, Daniel shot them. Shepherd agreed with Daniel's decision to kill them. He called the command center, "We are hit, we have a man down and two injured."

After a pause, the voice from the command center echoed, "Find and kill the targets."

After listening to this, Daniel was eagerly waiting to avenge Hill's death as he took charge of his unit. Even Shepard agreed to follow him. Daniel commanded, "Follow me! I will teach these motherfuckers a lesson today."

They all moved toward the crowded neighborhood. They followed Daniel to the place where they heard the last gunshots. It was a densely populated neighborhood, and the Marines moved forward with just one thing in mind—revenge. They spotted a house where they assumed that the fire had originated. Also, they thought that the targets were still hiding in there. It did not matter whether there were targets or not. The only thing that mattered was that they were so full of vengeance that this accumulated hatred transformed into a sinful act. While the insurgents had already crossed the neighborhood and were happy with their mission's success, the local people were dead scared. They knew something was coming to hunt them down. Daniel said, "Take positions, frag and clear."

They formed two groups and entered one of the houses. Daniel led the charge. The grenade created a noise that freaked out the children and women. They screamed with fear. Daniel fired with his assault rifle, thus killing everyone who was in his way. They searched and put bullets in dead bodies to ensure that no one survived. They searched every room and swept them clean. All those hiding behind closets were searched for and killed brutally—without even being given a chance to beg for mercy. Children who were hiding below the beds were also not spared. They were taken out of their hiding spots and shot multiple times. Not even the old citizens who were hiding were spared. They were executed similarly. One of the households' couples was scared and did not know how to react. The man held an Ak-47 rifle for defense. They both knew that the Marines were in no mood to spare anyone. He instructed his wife to stay low and not to come out—no matter what happened. She was so scared that she just kept quiet. Daniel and the others did not realize what they had just done as they were consumed by extreme rage. Overwhelming emotions sometimes make you do such unholy acts, but the human mind tends to ignore them until it is struck with a realization. The Iraqi man rushed toward the safe spot and was shot down by a sniper who was watching over the ally, assuming that he was one of the insurgents. The Marines thought that they had avenged their lost friend when the rush was over. However, they did not realize that there was someone who had survived this horrifying massacre— a young little girl. Although she was injured, she was spared by mistake or sheer luck. She was the only sole witness whom the Marines forgot to kill. She witnessed everything in all the houses and recorded the events. No one forgets such inhuman acts of requital. The Marines came out onto the street. They were thrilled by their action and were rejoicing over their victory, not realizing the enormity of the crime that they had just committed. Another Iraqi man ran toward the main street to ask for help, but a sniper had just shot him down as well. Daniel commanded the sniper not to engage any further through his communication devices. This made him think that he had done something that he should not have done. The woman came out running as her husband had just died for no reason. She was screaming in pain as her husband was lying dead in front of her. Daniel saw her mourning and tried to console her, but it was no use. It had already left a scar in Daniel's heart and it would not heal quickly. Shepard was not involved in the action, though he was proud of his men. He connected his coms and passed the message, "We have nailed down the targets."

After the beep, a voice was heard from the commanding officer. Jeremy said, "Well done, boys! You deserve a medal for your heroics!"

Shepard said, "Roger, Sir! Over and out."

"You heard the man! Let us go back, boys," said Captain Shepard.

Shepard addressed Daniel directly, "You handled yourself well. You went out there with courage. It's an act of valor."

Daniel felt very proud after listening to those words. It felt like an honor, but somewhere, he thought that whatever they had just done was barbaric. No brave man can kill women and children. Only a coward conducts such a low act. A Marine cannot even think of killing an unarmed civilian. All the Marines who departed the war crime scene, leaving behind the dead, were killed for no rhyme or reason. This was a war crime scene. Such is the ugly truth of collateral damage in modern warfare.

Seven years had passed since Daniel and his company was under heavy media coverage. The sole survivor of the Haditha incident narrated the event to the international media. Tanaz recorded her statement and the video footage of the entire incident. She eventually released the news in the media. She made allegations that were horrifying and detrimental to the US Marine corps and the whole of the US as a republic nation. She told the press that the Marines went inside the houses and killed everyone without blinking an eye.

The world saw the alleged crimes committed by the US Marines. There was immense international pressure on the United States Military. They had to act, or else these serious allegations could damage the image of all Marines and eventually sabotage the US on the international platform. All the accused the Marines were going through trials and Daniel knew that he would have to face the court-martial. Somewhere deep down, he knew what was coming. Before coming to Dimona, he got demoted to the rank of a private, and Daniel was explicitly given a punishment posting in Dimona, Israel. He was not ready to face his family and most importantly, he was clueless about what he would do after getting discharged from the military service. It was the job he had wanted to join since his childhood. How would he be able to live without his career? These insecurities and guilt were taking over his life. He did not know where he was heading—these questions had been bothering him for a long time.

Meanwhile, the political game of power was on a surge back in the US. The diplomats were awaiting such a golden opportunity to attack the ruling republicans. As soon as the media highlighted the Haditha case, John Muthra referred to the article published in Time magazine in 2005 which called the Marines *cold-blooded murderers.* This was damaging enough for the Marine Corps and put pressure on the investigating committee. The Marines Corps responded to such an allegation by stating that **the investigation was still ongoing and such remarks were derogatory and meaningless until the final analysis is closed.**

The statement made by the politician was a direct assault on the Marines. Daniel was under immense pressure from the investigation committee and the media. His family stayed with him during this disturbing time. He did not reveal the whole truth to them—how could he? He killed so many innocent people out of sheer rage. Honestly, he did not have the guts to face the truth. Linda responded, watching his husband in so much trouble, "Let us sue this man! He doesn't know anything you have been through."

Daniel did not say a word, but he was out of options. He just followed her wife's decision. Daniel filed a defamation suit against John Murtha for damaging his image and the Marines by accusing them of murders against Iraqi civilians.

After narrating the whole incident accurately to Diana, Daniel broke down. With tears of grief dripping, he said, "I haven't slept since the incident. I have these nightmares about those people whom I shot. I hear the screams of the innocent children who were crying in front of me—I can't get over this. I can't tell the truth to my family. What will I say to Jess, Liz and Linda?"

"They already know about this, Daniel," Diana interrupted Daniel. "You think you are the only one who has committed a crime in the very history of the armed forces? This is war, Son. You don't know who the enemy is, while the real enemy is mostly behind the scenes. You went out there to serve your country and do your job. That is your job— to protect your nation and its people. The innocent people you killed were mere pawns waiting to be crushed by some other forces. You can't imagine how countless innocent lives are affected in a war. When you joined the force to serve your nation, you were filled with motivation and patriotism. Still, when you got stuck in a tricky situation, you didn't understand the real enemy. Eventually, to avenge the fellow marine, you took innocent lives. Still, it was unintentional. You were just there at the wrong time! You didn't mean any harm, but your rage overtook your sense of perception. It happens during the war because war is a very complicated term. It has more complexities than a spider's web. It is like a maze. You never know what the next door could lead you to—maybe death or something you don't know about. You all could have died that day. You could have been in that Humvee instead of your mate."

Daniel listened to those statements very attentively. He never thought that he would hear such wise words ever—at least not in this place. He thought about it. Yeah! They could have all died that day. He could have been in that Humvee instead of Hill. He never looked at that incident in such a manner. He felt a little relieved after listening to Diana. He wanted her to tell her more about this, as he had never felt so comforted by anyone after that incident. He asked, "What I will tell my family? How will I be able to face them? They know I'm the culprit of this cowardly act, but what will I tell them? And how?"

"Tell them what you have told me and in the same manner. If I can understand, I'm sure they will also understand. They are your family, Daniel. They will have to understand," said the experienced Diana.

Daniel thought that she was not only a powerful woman but also a wise one as well. He did feel at ease now. He thought he would ask her the most challenging question that had been bothering him for a long time. He finally had the guts to ask her, "What will I do next? I mean, after the court-martial has declared me guilty of crimes, then what?"

"Well, there is nothing much I know about now, but I have something for you," replied Diana.

Daniel was listening very carefully. "You have to go to New York for that. There is a man I would like you to meet there. He will get you a job," said Diana in a commanding tone.

Daniel inquired, "Who is the man? And what kind of job?"

Diana replied, "You will soon know when the time is right. Just be patient. It won't be like your present job, but you will get a chance to serve people again and trust me, you will feel better."

Daniel felt better as he had something to look forward to at present. He felt so grateful that he did not know how to thank her. He said, "I don't know how to thank you for listening to my painful story. Not only that, but you are also trying to find me solace after my court-martial."

He broke down and thanked her again. Diana said, "You will be all right, Daniel. Don't let your past ruin your future. You cannot undo the past, but how you feel right now could change your future. So, you still have a choice. Always remember that."

Daniel thanked her and went to his room, but this time without any negative thoughts in his mind. He knew that there was still hope left in his life. He thought that he would never be able to pay back Diana for her efforts in putting him out of his misery. His punishment posting was almost over. It was time to face the court-martial, but Daniel was somewhat prepared to face the consequences in a better way. Diana came into Daniel's life as a ray of light that diminished his darkness. Dimona and Diana came as blessings in disguise for Private Daniel Ryan.

Finally, Daniel slept peacefully, while thinking of his family and a better future following an unknown journey. He was not thinking about the usual horrific incident for a change. After spending a few more days in peace, his time had arrived to move to the US. His luggage was packed. He had a final glimpse of the picture of his unit and decided to let the picture hang there. He was not ready to carry that baggage any further. He paid his tribute by saluting them while looking at his former fellow Marines. Before finally leaving the radar station, he thought of having a word with Diana. As he was about to knock on her office door, she appeared out of nowhere and said, "Looking for me, Soldier?"

Daniel smiled and said, "Yes, Ma'am."

Diana asked, "What brings you here? And before you leave, Daniel, take this with you." She gave him an envelope.

"What is in it, Ma'am?" asked Daniel curiously.

"It has something that will help you in the future," said Diana reluctantly.

Daniel understood the reference and did not say anything. He got emotional but tried to control himself. He saluted her in such a way that it seemed as if she was his commanding officer.

Diana just smiled and said, "Don't open it till your fate in the court-martial is decided. Good luck, Daniel!"

She just went to her office, and Daniel started ascending upwards along with a few others who were also about to leave after almost two months. He came to Dimona as a sad, grieving soldier, cribbing over his past and battling his inner conflicts. Diana helped him overcome them by having a small conversation. Sometimes just merely having a meaningful conversation with someone can release your troubled emotions and heavy burdens. Now, he was ready for any form of confrontation. He sat in convoy, holding together his family's picture and the letter that Diana had given him.

Chapter 3

The Family Affair

Daniel did not open the letter yet. While on his way to Jerusalem, he knew something in the letter was about his future. He remembered the incident of trials that began in December 2006 in which the US military filed charges against eight Marines, including Daniel and Joseph Farell. Daniel was charged with unpremeditated murder, which was a serious offense. During that time, the Marine corps had confirmed that none of the Iraqi civilians killed in the Haditha incident had been due to an IED explosion. This statement was enough to testify that the Marines committed a crime in Iraq. Further investigation would also reveal many detail-oriented findings and recorded reports that would help shape the future of the Marines. Daniel and his family, who had filed a defamation case against John Muthra, were not well received by the media. They were already chasing after his life for the ongoing trial for a long time. This accelerated the whole scenario more destructively. The suit made it worse. With the media making a mess of this story, Daniel was the one who was highlighted as the one accused of leading to the whole incident. Now the story was only whirling around Daniel. In the middle of this case, Farell testified against Daniel, stating that he had shot five Iraqi men who were sitting in the car near the street after the IED explosion. In retaliation, Daniel took them out of the car, shot them down one by one, and persuaded Captain Shepard to tell the commanding officer, Jeremy that those men were running away so that they had to take the shot under the rules of engagement. Farrell also claimed in his testimony that Daniel had such hatred against the Iraqis that he once claimed that he would teach them a lesson if they got hit by an IED. It was getting worse with each passing day. His family started having doubts, as Daniel kept quiet the whole time. Due to boundless pressure from the press and media, the defamation suit filed by Daniel was getting loosened up, as the whole world had already declared Daniel Ryan a war criminal. In 2009, the federal court dismissed the suit according to the principles laid down by the Westfall Act. No federal employee could be sued for personal conduct under their tenure. Daniel sensed that it was coming—his biggest fear was crawling in from all directions, and his family started to fear that he would not end it well. Society has its way of handling these issues around non-social behavior. Linda started facing much discrimination in her workplace. It was not enough. His daughters also faced the same kind of bullying at school. Daniel thought about how one wrong decision could cost him. It cost him greatly. What Daniel and his company did back in Iraq started to manifest into an abominable course a few years back. You can run away from yourself but not from your destiny. His running was not over yet. He knew his family was placed in a testing time, and he was failing them miserably. He did not have the guts to justify the horrific incident. One evening, Linda came home feeling upset about something. She was annoyed with her colleagues for criticizing her husband for murder. She angrily said, "These people have no right to accuse you until the investigation is over. I have spoken to Dad. You need to answer a few questions before it destroys us all. What will happen to our daughters? Their future is at stake. You need to do something about it."

Daniel was listening to her carefully and tried to calm her down. He said, "Whatever you say, I'm ready to do it."

Daniel was distraught and angry after spending time with his daughters, who also narrated what happened in school. He thought that he could not avoid confrontation anymore. He had to act now, or it would be too late to rebuild everything. He had to protect his family. After a few days, he decided that his family members should give an interview that would directly impact the American audience, to which Linda agreed. She also convinced her father, who gave an interview in which they requested the Americans to be patient and wait until the investigation was completed. Daniel fully briefed them to remind the Americans to remain patient until the investigation was over. His father said, "We are 100 percent behind you, Son."

After the interview was over, it did not have much of an impact as Daniel had expected because the people were furious with the situation. He decided after thinking a lot that he had to face the media once and for all, though he was not allowed as per the Military rules. He consulted a few of his senior colleagues who were non-judgmental and unbiased. They told him that he could speak to the media as Daniel was not in active service. Still, they told him to consider some factors such as non-leakage of any information, no unlawful remarks, and being highly apologetic for gaining maximum sympathy. In speaking to one of the Reuters journalists, Daniel said that he was sorry for losing the children and women in Iraq. Still, he would do the same thing again if he faced the same combat situation. After that interview, the media raised more questions than the answers that they got. It all seemed to get worse for Staff Sergeant Daniel Ryan. He did this to protect his family and the family backed Daniel until the truth was not revealed. In 2006, in an ongoing Military investigation, Daniel's Commanding officer, Jeremy and Captain Shepard of the third battalion were dismissed from their duties due to suspicion—of being involved in the Haditha incident. There was not much progress on the investigation front. This was the first act of punishment that started the digging into the Marine corps of the Haditha incident. The higher the stature of your rank, the higher the catastrophic impact, which is also known as collateral damage.

Jerusalem Israel 2010

Suddenly, the troops' convoy was stopped at the Jerusalem Military Airport. Daniel decided that he would finally tell Linda, Jess, and Liz the truth— and not just them, but the whole world. He was done running. He had agreed to plead guilty. However, he did not know how his family would receive that news and what would happen after they knew the whole truth behind the incident, which was tearing Daniel's world apart. Diana's words were still echoing in his mind. He thought that they had the right to know, and they would have to understand. He was ready to let go, no matter what happened in the court-martial trials. Daniel departed from Israel forever in the US Military aircraft, carrying the soldiers back to their home soil. It had been a relatively life-changing experience in Dimona. He was pleased to leave for Connecticut. He remembered an incident from his past…

After Joseph Farrell's testimony, it became tough for Daniel to cope with the trial. Farrell's remarks acted as fuel for an already fired-up situation. Daniel was again summoned into the court for the ongoing investigation. He did not know how to report everything to the investigation officer. His family situation was in a deep mess—he was off duty and the press was the icing on the cake. The officer called him in shortly. Daniel, fully dressed in his Marine uniform, entered and saluted the investigating officer. Lieutenant Colonel Peter Hawk was in charge of Daniel's case. He acknowledged his presence and said, "At ease, Staff Sergeant."

Daniel was restless and worried. His body language could be well understood and Peter noted it. He asked, "So, will you tell me what happened in Haditha?"

After taking a deep breath, Daniel gathered himself and said, "Sir, they were trying to flee the crime scene after they triggered the IED and we were out of options. We had to engage."

"You want me to believe this bullshit? Do you think I'm one of those Americans who doesn't give a shit? I have seen more warfronts than you ever did. I know what causes this manslaughter. So do not take me for some regular media guy wanting some informative juice to earn a living, I'm a soldier just like you and you will tell me what happened out there, fact by fact, event by event. Is that clear, Officer? And what the hell were you thinking—talking to media like that? Will you do the same shit again? For that, you have to remain in the Marine Corps. I have many witnesses and evidence against you, so you better stop wasting my time and start talking without fabrication. And do remember, Captain

Shepard and Lieutenant Colonel Jeremy are not there anymore to save you here."

Daniel was taken aback for a moment. He was damn scared now, but he decided to speak after analyzing and recalling how his family was bullied a few days back. "They killed Hill, Sir. I collected his body parts. They always killed us from behind. This time, I decided to go behind them…the so-called people you are trying to protect," replied Daniel with some of the courage left in his voice.

"Two women and five children—what harm could they have done?" asked Peter confidently.

"They were caught up in the line of fire, and…"

"Bullshit," screamed Peter interrupting him. "I told you to tell me the truth and just the truth. This is your last chance."

Daniel took another deep breath and after a momentary pause, he said, "I killed them, Sir, not my unit. I didn't want to kill them. It just happened. Things got out of hand, and we lost control. I did it, Sir. I'm guilty of these crimes and I'm sorry."

Daniel froze for a few moments as though he had lost control of time, and remained extremely silent without twitching his eyes. After a brief moment of silence, Peter said, "Hmmm, now you are on track."

Daniel did not say a word after reliving that horrifying memory again. Peter said, "You are dismissed."

Daniel got up, saluted the Colonel, and returned to his lawyer. Daniel told his lawyer what had happened in the courtroom. His lawyer was utterly disappointed in him. "I told you to deny all the charges. What is wrong with you? You are finished now, Daniel. It's over. Go home and tell Linda the same," said Hedrick.

Daniel thought Hedrick was right. It would cost him a lot, but he was out of options—the fears had gotten over his mind. Now he was more worried about the whole episode. After the court was dismissed, he went to his New London, Connecticut home. After Daniel left,

Lieutenant Colonel Peter Hawk understood under what circumstances Daniel had taken that decision. Ultimately, he could not save him and keep him in the force as well, but he decided to reduce his pain. Peter had all the pieces of evidence and witness statements through Tenaz's research report on how Daniel and his team committed the crime. Still, as a soldier, he thought it was his duty to state the facts of the incident. At the same time, he understood Daniel's situation. So, he decided to issue a statement. A few days passed. It was becoming more difficult for Daniel with each passing day. He thought that he should see a therapist as he desperately needed to talk to someone who would be unbiased. After coming from a short run, Daniel reached his home, feeling that he was losing all hope. Every time he entered the home, he tried to smile a fake just for everyone to realize that everything was normal. He was drowning deep inside his mind. He sat on his couch and played with his daughter as if nothing had happened. Jess and Liz were too small to understand what was going on with their father, but they were the only reason for his happiness. Liz took the remote and turned on the television. Linda also joined them. There was breaking news on one of the channels and it was related to the trial of a Marine. Daniel thought it had begun formally, and decided just to have a glimpse of the TV headlines. He thought of switching off the TV. But he was curious to know what progress happened in the case. In the breaking news, it was mentioned that Lieutenant Colonel Peter had just released his statement regarding the ongoing investigation against the Marines under the charge of the Article 32 hearing. He said, "Charges against Staff Sergeant Daniel Ryan should be considered as negligent homicide, not in terms of murder of two women and five children. The murder charges should be dropped." He further stated, "After going through the shreds of evidence and carefully scrutinizing the facts, there was no intention to kill that can be levied upon Staff Sergeant Ryan. Hypothetically if a Marine fails to conduct his duties properly and gets involved in civilian casualties, the charges of negligent homicide are applicable, not murder. There is no presence of strong intent of murder beyond a reasonable doubt. The witness will have a biased opinion."

The whole Ryan family watched and listened very carefully, but Daniel's daughter did not seem to understand the seriousness of the matter. However, Linda was a little angry at Daniel. It was both good news and bad news. As a Marine, Daniel was a relieved man, but things were about to get nasty as a husband. Linda told the children to go upstairs. They were not in the mood to go as it was not bedtime yet. Linda raised her voice, "I said go upstairs now."

Daniel knew what was coming. He also told the children to listen to their mother. They reluctantly went upstairs. As soon as the children left, Linda dominantly asked, "What is this supposed to mean? What the hell is going on?"

Daniel remained quiet. "I asked you a question," repeated Linda.

After a few moments of silence, Daniel replied, "It was an accident."

"What the hell! What was an accident?" Linda was furious now.

"The explosion distracted us, and we accidentally pulled out our triggers. It was unintentional, just a response action," Daniel said without fuss.

"Accident? Do you think I will believe this crappy story of yours? And suppose I believed this story for a moment. So what? You have killed little children and women, you ruthless man. You call yourself a Marine?" Linda was distraught, and why would she not be?

Daniel tried to control things by trying to hold her. "Relax, Linda, it was an accident and nothing else."

"Get your hands off me. What happened to Dan? Who the hell are you? Are you the man whom I loved? Who is this man?" asked Linda, sobbing.

"Trust me, I did not kill them. They killed Hill. He died right in front of me," said Daniel reassuringly.

Those words were of no use to console the hurt Linda. She spoke, "So you say these women and children killed Hill? Great job avenging Hill, Dan! Well done! Have you ever thought about the age of the children whom you had killed? Damn it! They are the same as Jess. You are insane! You are not the same person I used to know."

These lines made them more uncomfortable. Daniel fell onto his couch and started crying. Daniel sobbed and told Linda not to tell the children about it. Linda kept quiet and went to her room. Daniel thought he was finished now. The only silver lining in these darkest hours was the charges he was facing were dropped. It was still bearable to be an incapable soldier who did not perform his duties as per the rules rather than being called a cold-blooded murderer.

The aircraft landed at the Marine Corps base camp at Pendleton Oceanside, California, the headquarters for Daniel's Regiment—Third Battalion First Marines. He had to catch a flight to Connecticut the following day to return home. It was a long journey, but he was prepared for the circus following whatever had happened. Reporting back to his headquarters, he was dismissed and allowed to go. He remembered how thrilled he once was to join the battlefield of Afghanistan. He was indeed a brave soldier, but sometimes life teaches you lessons in unimaginable ways—just to make you aware that you are actually in charge of what happens within you. What happens externally is mostly not within your control. You always have a choice to at least choose what happens within you. Daniel could not control his emotions when the outside situation took over his body and mind, which came out of rage. His mind was full of vengeance against the Iraqis. He committed such an act that he never thought he could ever execute. He could have reacted differently. He could have carried out a sweep to ensure the insurgents were captured without hurting civilians. We always have a choice, and so did Daniel, but he chose what would haunt him for the rest of his life.

He boarded the flight to Connecticut. While on his way back home on the flight, he remembers another incident that occurred a few years ago. Once the charges of murder were dropped, which he was not expecting at all, he tried to contact Colonel Peter unofficially. He wanted to thank him for the sympathy that he showed him by reducing his dent of shame and disgrace from his uniform. He paid a visit to the Colonel's house. Peter was expecting Daniel someday, which indeed happened. Peter welcomed him, and Daniel was surprised by the gesture. Peter said, "I knew you would come to see me someday."

Daniel saluted Peter, and responded, "At ease, Soldier, this is not the court-martial. This is my home. Sit."

He requested Daniel to be seated and feel comfortable. Daniel just sat down quietly. He was not anticipating this welcome. They were both sitting on the couch in his living room. Peter offered Daniel a drink, to which Daniel did not respond but eventually took the glass full of scotch. Peter asked, "So tell me, why are you here, Staff Sergeant?"

Daniel said, "I just wanted to thank you for your faith in me by dropping those charges. It helped my family and me in numerous ways. We are all very grateful to you…and I don't know how to repay you."

Peter did not say anything for a few minutes. After a while, he said, "I may have dropped the charges of murder, but the way I see this, you will be discharged from the Marine Corps…I'm sorry, but I can't promise you anything. As a Marine myself, I must serve the US and its people. I know exactly what you and the others did there…I can't save you—no one can. I can only make this poison spread slowly."

These words penetrated the heart of Staff Sergeant Daniel Ryan. He knew he would be dismissed one day, but still, he had to thank his superior. Dan asked, "I know, Sir, what's coming, but still, there must be a way out of this mess or to slow the process."

After thinking for a while, Peter came up with a solution and said, "By slowing this down, you mean you don't want to go to jail or something else. Be specific, Staff Sergeant."

Daniel's worst nightmare was to end up in a prison cell. It was the most unfavorable situation ever for a Decorated Soldier. He knew he had committed a severe crime, but Peter wanted him to be ready to go to prison. Dan thought he would take his life instead of facing such disgrace. He was somehow hoping to avoid imprisonment at any cost. After analyzing that situation, he said, "Yes, Sir, that is exactly what

I meant. I don't think any soldier would like to. Help me, Sir. I will manage the rest somehow."

"You will not be able to manage anything because there won't be anything left to work on, Daniel. You will lose your job and much more. Though I have something in my mind, you will have to sacrifice your rank for that. Are you ready to let go of that?" asked Peter firmly.

Daniel thought about his rank. After thinking for a few more minutes, he understood it would be an official demotion. He enquired by saying, "What will it be?"

"A Private," said Peter.

Daniel was disheartened and disappointed after listening to the word *Private*. He thought he would be a Private again, but he was not ready to accept the fact that he would be addressed as a Private. What about the medals and rank that he had earned as a soldier? He felt destroyed just by listening to this idea. Then, he thought he would still be spared from prison. He was still not ready to accept that consequence. After all, he was a brave Marine. He somehow nodded.

Peter said, "I know…it won't be easy to get and digest it…but it's a fact. What you have done comes with a cost. You should have thought this through. You should have thought this before opening fire on those innocent children and women, Daniel. In comparison to that, it's bloody nothing. Imagine the loss that they had to suffer due to your one irresponsible move. Don't forget that and come to terms with reality. The sooner, the better for you. The least you can do is accept the punishment gracefully. Still, you will live and…yeah, there is more. You will also receive a pay cut—be ready for that. So, are you ready?"

Daniel recalled the incident again and thought, *yes*. What Peter was suggesting was the right move. He said, "Yes, Sir. I accept it, all of it."

Peter also appreciated the move by saying that he talked with the right approach. "Lastly, to avoid your time in prison, I have one more thing in mind," he said.

Daniel thought that he would suggest going to hell for the rest of his life. He reluctantly said, "What would that be, Sir?"

"You must go somewhere in the Gulf region for a few months to avoid your prison time," said Peter.

Daniel thought it would be the price that he had to pay by living abroad. He asked, "Which place, Sir?"

"You will know soon enough. Just do as I tell you to do, I can't save you completely, but I can make a few arrangements to ease you down," said Peter comfortingly.

Daniel thought for a moment and realized that he was out of options. The only way out of this was by completely trusting Colonel Peter. "Sir, as you say," said Daniel.

Peter told him that he would be instructed as per the procedure. "Sir, one last thing, my lawyer will drop my case as I accept your proposal. Then, I will not have any counsel for the remaining procedure," said Daniel.

"This was bound to happen. Don't worry, you will have someone for that," said Peter.

After the tough talk, he left to return home. On his way back, he was still trying hard to come to terms with the chaotic path that Peter had asked him to follow.

New London US 2010

The onboarding flight announcement about the upcoming landing at the Groton Airport woke Daniel up after a long nap. The flight was about to land at the New London home of Private Daniel Ryan. Daniel had been through a lot as a man, but justice was yet to be served for being a soldier. After Dimona, he faced challenges and experiences which were similar to being confined within a prison cell, but he was counseled well by Diana. He was mentally ready to face the trial but unsure about his family's situation. That was the only question that was now troubling him. He reached his home. He saw Linda talking to someone on her cell phone outside, but he was ready to face the world through Diana's efforts. He did not know how she would look at him after months without much contact. Linda was deeply engrossed in the telephonic conversation. She did not notice that her husband had just reached home after traveling more than a thousand miles. Daniel did not bother distracting her. He headed straight toward the main door. As soon as he entered, he was greeted by his daughters, Elizabeth and Jessica. They screamed in joy after looking at their father after so long. They called out to their father by yelling "Dad!" and it was audible outside. Linda ran straight inside, thinking that the children had turned on the TV. There was no news of court-martial updates. She was very concerned about her children and what impact they could have on them. She was a little astonished to see her husband and for a moment, she ignored the facts about the trial that was in her mind and ran toward her husband. Forgetting everything and hugging him, she broke down and embraced him—so did Dan. It was a happy moment for the Ryans. After settling down, Dan sat on his favorite spot on the staircase. Linda saw him and sat down next to him. They both never got some time alone since the incident began. He was about to ask her something, but Linda asked, "How was jail, Dan?"

Daniel was utterly outraged after listening to this question. He tried to calm himself down for a moment but could not. He raised his voice and said, "What does that mean? I wasn't in jail. Where is this coming from? Who is giving these stupid ideas?"

In a very relaxed manner, Linda said, "Calm down, Dan. The children are sleeping…Hasn't your anger caused enough damage already?"

After listening to her, he felt broken but did try to calm himself. He chose silence rather than replying to such allegations from his wife.

Linda was also quiet for a moment, and then she decided to break the silence by saying, "If you weren't in jail, then where were you?"

Dan did not say anything, but Dan being Dan asked her a counter-question, "Where are you getting this information?"

Linda confidently replied, "I have my sources."

"Since when did you become a spy?" asked Daniel sarcastically.

Linda did not answer.

After some time, she got up and started going inside. Before leaving, she said, "Hendrik told me everything, Dan. You lied to me, your family, and your country. You think people won't know about your evil deeds. You were in an Israeli prison somewhere. How did you get demoted to a Private? Your bank balance has been reduced. You are a failure and disgrace to Marine Corps. I know everything, Dan," said Linda trying to control her tears.

Daniel felt his heart pierced by a thousand bullets fired simultaneously from every possible direction. He remembered Diana and what she had told him, "If I can understand, they will understand—they have to."

However, what Diana had said did not happen. It was exactly the opposite. After gathering his strength, he said, "You know what, Hendrik told you everything correctly except for the jail part."

He stood up and went for a walk alone. He returned after an hour and found Linda on the phone again. He knew it was Hendrik…whom she had talked to for hours. He knew Hendrik was feeding ideas into her mind but could not do anything. Dan had never felt such helplessness in his entire life. He started doubting her. She was probably getting close to Hendrik and having an affair.

Chapter 4

The Broken Man

Things were not going as per plan for Daniel and Diana, though it was happening as per Peter's script. The whole trial saga was minimized for the most part. Many charges were dropped from the Marines. Peter did his work well and saved the US military's image. He managed the situation so well that the Marines Corps praised him. Only the final act was to be ordered—probably the most painful one for Daniel. Peter kept his promise. He did not let Daniel go to prison by initiating a move to Dimona, though that information was classified and off the record. Hendrik was scratching every bit of information that he could find on Dan. According to his informant, Daniel was kept in prison, and Dan testified to this by telling Linda that he was indeed in Israel. Everyone thought he was in jail. By the terms of the agreement, Daniel could never talk to anyone about the radar station, or the remaining things would also start falling apart. Linda believed that he was indeed kept in prison. No one could ever know where Daniel had been for the past few months, except for a handful of people. Daniel had a few expectations from Linda after Dimona, but they went away. Dan became insecure about Linda. He thought of paying a visit to Hendrik, but he wanted confirmation about his doubts. To his surprise, he started observing her behavior and spying on her, but he did not find any substantial evidence against her. Maybe he was just a true and honest lawyer, who was faithful to his client. However, it did not make any significant improvement to their relationship. Dan was concerned about his daughters and their future as they were affected by this mess. He somehow knew that after the court-martial, he would try again to rebuild his family from scratch, but observing the sudden changes in Linda, he was unsure how to do it.

The daughters loved Dan. It was just a phase, and it would pass. They would all be as they were once before. These were Dan's thoughts—to make him understand that everything would be all right. Lieutenant Colonel Peter Hawk called Daniel to the Military court again. Daniel woke up and got dressed in his uniform. He thought maybe, that day was his military career's last day. He always remembered Diana a lot, as she was the only positive influence on him. He remembered her every word carefully. It gave him the strength to move on with Haditha. He reached the court. There was no need for Hendrik as he had already refused to take Daniel's case after his non-denial charges. Private Daniel Ryan was called in quickly. He went inside, saluted the officers, and did not even gaze upon them by keeping his eyes low. Peter said, "At ease. This is Commander Wisbender."

Peter pointed at the most senior person of the central command. "Sit down, Daniel," said Peter.

"How was your leap of faith?" Peter asked about Dimona.

"Sir, it was life-changing," said Daniel.

"I'm sure it was. I have all the reports now. The media is not paying attention to you anymore. Now, the final part, are you ready for it?" asked Peter authoritatively.

Daniel thought Peter said that he would not be discharged from the Marine Corps. He had been out of options since the incident took place in 2005. He was still being thrown here and there like a football. He lost control over many things. Daniel remembered Diana again and after a few seconds, he said, "Sir, I think I am."

Peter and Wisbender were observing his body language closely. They thought that as a man in his situation, he was doing decently. Most of the other members facing trial on the same charges were either broken or taking some serious therapy. No matter how strong you pretend to be from the inside, you cannot hide your true emotions since your feelings will be reflected by defying body language. Daniel was somewhat calm. Diana and her wisdom were the only factors that were keeping him going.

Peter and Wisbender started discussing something about an agreement, which made Daniel a little curious, but he could not say anything. After a brief discussion, Peter turned his attention straight toward Daniel and offered him a file. Daniel took it immediately without hesitating. In a casual tone, Peter said, "This is an agreement upon which you have accepted dereliction in the field of duty and your plea of being guilty in this court."

Daniel was amazed by Peter's statement and said, "But Sir, I haven't… How can you say that, with due respect, Sir? Neither did I disobey any order, nor am I an inefficient soldier on duty, Sir."

"Daniel, when did we say that you were an incapable soldier? As far as negligence is concerned, this is the only way to save you from a dishonorable discharge and most importantly, from charges like homicide and manslaughter. And don't forget our contribution to saving you from jail. This is the only option you have left us with—accept it and save yourself. You will not be honored, but you won't be dishonored as well. You will get a general discharge from the military with honorable conditions. It's the only option you have left us, Private Daniel Ryan," said Lieutenant General Wisbender.

Daniel remembered that Hill's body was lying in pieces near the destroyed Humvee. He remembered Diana's words, "You could have been there instead of Hill. God has given you a second chance. Let's not waste it. Appreciate it, accept it and move on with it. Remember Daniel, we all have a choice. We can't undo the past, but what we feel within us, in this very moment is determined by you and no one else. What you chose that day has landed you here. What you choose next could take you somewhere else—maybe someplace better or worse. So, choose wisely and no one can take this right away from a human being."

Daniel closed his eyes, and suddenly he had a feeling that he was ready for it. He did not realize how this thought manifested in his mind, but he was ready. He read the agreement and said, "I plead guilty, Sir!"

Peter and Wisbender were left speechless and stunned but were happy that a new journey was about to begin for him. Daniel thought he would tell Linda what had happened at Haditha, exactly, honestly, and without hesitating, though he thought it was too late for her to understand now. There was a huge communication gap between the couple. Daniel would be convicted for *dereliction of duty* and would soon receive the *General Discharge* from the Marine Corps as per the agreement. He stood up and saluted his superior for maybe the last time and walked with a certain calmness on his face. He headed straight toward his home and rushed to tell his family about what would happen officially.

He reached home from the military court and was expecting Linda to be there. Indeed, she was waiting for him there, but the children were missing. Dan addressed her and said, "Linda, I want to tell you something important."

Linda remained quiet and later said, "Even I want to tell you something, and it's also damn important."

Daniel did not know what was coming. He insisted, "Yeah, go ahead! Tell me."

Linda replied, "You begin first."

Daniel had no clue what Linda wanted to tell him. He thought maybe he was right about Hendrik and her.

Daniel was prepared to face this but thought of telling her what he had decided at court. "Back in Iraq, we were attacked by insurgents. They planted a bomb on the road, it exploded, and Hill didn't survive. I was full of hatred and vengeance after seeing hill's dead body. I lost control—the feeling of revenge consumed me and I let my team follow me into the unknown. It was not the first time a marine had died in such a cowardly act in my presence. I was determined that if something happened that day, they would pay for it this time, and it did. I went into homes and killed everyone who encountered me, including women and children. I didn't realize that what I had done there was a cowardly act, and I regret it every moment of my life, even after nearly seven years. This is the exact truth—of what happened there and I was saved by my superiors, who still gave me a chance," said Daniel, feeling relieved that he had told her about one of the deepest griefs he had stored in his mind.

There was absolute silence in the living room. Linda was processing the whole thing. She sat down immediately, realizing that it was her husband behind the manslaughter. She broke down. Dan tried to console her, but she said, "Don't you touch me, I was right about you. It was you this whole time—acting innocent. You are a monster, Dan. Marine Corps may forgive you, but I won't. I thought you did kill those innocent children by accident. I never thought it was you who deliberately shot them. You coward! Everyone was right this whole time. It was me who still believed in you—thinking that maybe it was an accident."

Her cries turned louder. She was hurt, of course. Why would she not be hurt? She was kept in the dark. She knew he did something wrong but never thought it was Dan who lied to her the whole time. He was indeed responsible for killing innocent Iraqi citizens.

Dan kept quiet. Somehow, he knew this was coming. He said, "I know I lied to you, but I didn't have the strength. I didn't tell you or anybody for that matter. I know you will not understand—maybe it's too late. I'm sorry I hurt you and the children. I let all of you down."

"Yes, you have let us down. I don't want my children to be with someone who is a cold-blooded killer—a God-damned son of a bitch! You will always remain a murderer to me and you know what, even if you had never told me all this, I would have left you…Here, go through this now," she threw a file at Dan's face and left for work.

Dan sat down quietly after gathering the papers that were scattered on the floor. They were divorce papers. Dan never saw that coming. He was utterly broken. He thought that she would be angry and had all the right to be angry, but this was not right. He felt…maybe she was going away with Hendrik and playing the blame game on him. His doubts manifested into something else now. She would have left him—whether he told her the truth or not. Daniel was furious but could not do anything as his crime was more severe. Daniel still doubted her but never dared to confront her. He wanted to dig deep into that…He was too wrapped in guilt and shame. He thought that even if she was going away, he had no right to intervene. It was too late in every possible manner. He had screwed up—he knew he had. He took the divorce documents and now he had two files to read that night. He took a bottle of Scottish Whiskey along with it.

He opened his closet, took out his licensed Glock pistol, and saw a frame lying in a corner. He took it out, the frame contained the medals and awards he had received during his military career. There were seven medals received by him in all. One of the medals was for good conduct. He broke down. He heard a sound. He saw Linda packing her stuff in the bedroom. He could not do anything. He was holding a pistol. He hid the gun in his pajamas. He asked, "Where are the children?"

Linda replied, "They are at a place where they are supposed to be. Read the divorce papers carefully, and I will see you in court."

She left without adding anything else. Daniel was left alone to face all of the problems by himself. His military career was about to get over, his wife and children left him, and his wife was probably having an affair. He thought he was now left with nothing. He did not know where he was heading. He was left with no motive to carry on.

He went back to his room and opened the file. As per the divorce documents, it was clear that he was not given custody of his daughters, though he would be given a chance to meet them every month. Daniel kept the files aside. Now was the time to read about *dereliction of duty*. In the plea agreement, charges of assault and manslaughter were not seen anywhere. It only mentioned that Daniel did not perform his task as per the military rules.

Now, Dan had to sign both agreements. What a turnaround of events! Dan thought. At one moment, he was a Staff Sergeant serving his country, and in the next, he was about to be discharged from the Marine Corps. On top of that, his family had abandoned him to face everything alone. He took out the frame again and saw his medals. He was continuously drinking and the bottle was almost about to get over. He thought of calling Shepard but did not. It was over for him. He realized that it was finished for him. He took out his pistol and was about to take his life. He pointed the gun toward himself and was about to pull the trigger. Suddenly, he remembered the letter given by Diana in Dimona a few months ago. He dropped his weapon down and kept it aside. He walked toward his closet, searched for that letter, and found it. He remembered Diana again when she said, "Don't open the letter till your fate in the court is finalized."

Dan thought it was about time. He opened the letter. There was an address of New York and a name—Dr. Neil Francis. He thought he would visit Dr. Francis and then pull the trigger, as he had nothing to live for anymore. Dan dozed off on the sofa and held the letter and the gun in the other hand.

Dan just kept waiting for the next few days. With each passing day, it became unbearable for him to cope with the emotional trauma that he was going through. Everything seemed to be over for him, and he thought of seeking therapy because he wanted to interact with someone. Damn! He missed Dimona—the most unlikely place one can imagine. He thought of calling Diana, but it was impossible as it was the unofficial location with no access. He remembered how Peter made agreements for Dimona—it was a classified location. Dan signed a pact not to utter the word Dimona in front of anyone—not even to his family. It was off the record—as if it never happened. It was all crafted to erase Daniel from the trials and prison. He went through the divorce and discharged files many times. He had already accepted all of it.

Meanwhile, Linda shifted to her parent's house along with her daughters. Elizabeth and Jessica were still unable to accept her mother's decision to leave their father. Linda, however, made sure that the children did not get affected by that decision, but it was not going to happen her way. The least she could do was never tell them about the last conversation Dan had with her, knowing it would disturb them deeply. These traumatizing events lead to further mental issues, especially amongst growing children, as their brains are still developing. She only told them that it became impossible for her to stay with him, mainly due to a lack of understanding and differences in opinion. His long court trial and reduced pay were the major significant topics in the divorce plea. Indeed, it was affecting their lives personally and financially. There was no Hendrik in her life. She extracted all the information from him to keep a tab on the ongoing investigation. As a lawyer, Hendrik did all he could to help her as his client. He told her how Dan accepted the murder charges of killing those children and women. He further stated that there was no scope left for winning the case. It was all over. He provided vital information to Linda, who had doubts about her husband as he was not behaving normally. She knew he was hiding stuff regarding the Haditha incident, thus making her even more curious. She tried to help him and arranged an interview which got messed up. She trusted him all her life and Dan only lied to her from the beginning of the massacre. Even Linda and her father supported Dan by asking for support on national television. She tried to do everything possible to stabilize and save that relationship. She thought it was better to live alone than to live with him as he did not remain the same as before. She was only concerned about her children's future and nothing else. She never thought about another man. Linda knew that Dan's court-martial news would reach her children one day. It was better to prepare them than give them false hope. She did everything to protect her daughters from the world.

On the other hand, Dan was heading to New York, in search of an unknown man. His fate in the court-martial was decided, but there was some time left in it. His family's fate was also fixed and agreed upon, but it had some time. However, the outcome had already been determined. A few pleasantries separated these situations, and the official announcement was awaited. Dan knew it was unavoidable now, so he wanted to see what life had in store for him on the other side. He knew no future was left for him in Connecticut—he had to move out. So, he embarked on his new journey, and so did Linda because she never imagined such a situation arising in her life, where she would have to live without Dan. She got a middle-level hierarchy job as a creative head in product development at a marketing company. She was going to test her writing and marketing skills. Her experience as a blogger also added value to her current job entitlement.

Chapter 5

Rebuilding from Scratch

A bus stopped at the New York Metropolitan Station. Dan reached his destination. The address mentioned in the letter, which was received by Diana was New York-Presbyterian Hospital, one of the oldest hospitals in New York City. Dan thought, *what will a Marine do in a hospital?* Maybe he could assist a patient or who knows. However, he left aside his past and wanted to know more about this letter. He reached the hospital and enquired about Dr. Neil Francis at the main reception. The receptionist called someone on the phone. Dan just waited and started looking at the hospital, while observing the patients and staff moving around in this busy place. He thought again, *what will I do here?* He thought he could be an assistant. Yes, he could do that. The receptionist requested, "Please show me your ID."

Dan quickly gave her a military ID card. He thought, *why not hand over the recommendation letter to her?* He said, "Take this and please show this to Dr. Francis."

She took it and glanced at it. The letter was on New York-Presbyterian Hospital's official letterhead. She immediately contacted an assistant and handed over the document. "Give it to Dr. Neil," instructed Monica.

She asked Dan to wait for a while, and he would be called. Dan followed the instruction and sat quietly in the corner next to the reception. He thought there was no place for him there. He would suffocate in such a tense environment. He needed to talk to someone desperately. He waited there for hours and thought of taking a nap. Suddenly, he fell asleep, and Monica called out his name, "Mr. Daniel Ryan, please wake up!"

She had to push Daniel to wake him from his nap. "Dr. Neil will see you now. Please follow me," she said.

Dan gathered himself and followed Monica. They took the lift. The gate opened on the fifth floor. She pointed at the chamber of Dr. Francis. Dan acknowledged that and went toward the door. Before knocking, he saw the description hanging on the door—*Dr. N. Francis, Head of the Cardiology.*

"Come in," a voice said from inside.

Dan went in, followed his military procedures, and was about to salute the doctor instead of greeting him. He soon realized that he was not at court. He quickly rectified it by saying, "Good afternoon, Doctor."

Dr. Francis was an older man with a grey mustache. He wore glasses and closely watched something on his computer. He stared at Dan and said, "Relax, Daniel. It's not your army's court. Please sit down. I will be there with you in a moment."

Dan looked around his chamber. It was a big cabin. He was one of the most reputed cardiologists in the city. His appointment schedule was elaborate since at least two of his assistants were always busy scheduling his appointments. Dan thought, *how the hell did Diana know this man?* Then he thought Diana was indeed someone very resourceful. Dan's attention was all over the place as he was busy observing all the awards and recognition certificates he had received in his lifetime. A wall of fame was decorated with awards, honors, and newspaper articles. Dr. Francis asked, "So Daniel, I'm sorry something or the other keeps coming up…I knew you would come here one day. Diana told me about you…Sorry about your court marital."

Dan was surprised by the statement. He thought that the doctor knew way too much about him. He was just about to introduce himself. Dan hesitated a bit, and then he asked, "Thank you, Doctor. If I may ask with your permission, how do you know so much about me? I mean, how do you know Diana Ma'am?"

Dr. Francis smiled at Dan looked at his assistants, and said, "Thomas, Joe give us a moment alone."

Dan thought it was otherwise significant; why would he ask his assistants to leave randomly? They both got up and stepped outside the cabin. As soon as they left, Dr. Francis said, "Well, just for you to know, Diana is my wife. She works for the CIA. I thought you knew all this. Didn't she tell you?"

Dan was taken aback. He thought, *what the hell!* He never thought of this. Yes, Diana *Francis* was her name—how could he forget such minute details? It was always written right in front of his eyes all the time. He looked at that door more than a thousand times back in Dimona. He was awestruck but was thrilled by this detail. He said, "No, Doctor, she only speaks about whatever is needed."

Dr. Francis smiled and said, "Yes, you are right about this. Israel is her last assignment, I hope. So, tell me something, how was Israel?"

Dan said, "It was like hell…It was too much for a radar station."

Dr. Francis laughed and said, "Do you think it was a radar station?"

Dan got terrified but ignored it. "It's more than that, but I can't tell you more…She is about to finish the task there, and she will be here soon…well, will be coming back to you. I have given it a thought, but you need to sort out the mess. I'm sorry about it…There is a post of a security officer, which is vacant at the moment, and your profile matches the requirement. I know you are over-experienced for this job and how you feel about it, but this is the only offer I have now…and…"

Dan interrupted Dr. Francis. "I'd love to do some real job. It's about time. Count me in, Doctor," said Dan in a rush.

Dr. Francis was not surprised. Diana had briefed him well before that meeting. He said, "I'm glad that you are very interested in the job, but again, let your trial be over. You're good to go…Free to join us."

Daniel smiled. He was happy to have an opportunity to start over again, although from scratch. Still, he was not expecting anything after what happened in Dimona and Haditha. It made him feel content. He replied, "Don't worry about the court-martial. It will be over soon, Doctor, maybe within this month, but there is one more thing that I would like to bring to your attention. It's about my personal life…I'm going through a separation. I know how it will end…I might need another favor from you. Could you recommend a therapist for me? I need to start afresh without carrying any baggage on my journey. So, if you could please…"

"Of course, Daniel, why not! I liked that you opened up about it. I appreciate your honesty…and I would love to help. Next time, just come back here. I will put you up with Patricia. She is the best in the business these days."

Dan was grateful to God for meeting Diana in his life. He thought it was over, but somehow life wanted Daniel to move on with it. He cheerfully got up and said before leaving, "Thank you so much, Doctor. I'm thankful to you both. I don't know how I will be able to repay you two…I was in a mess and you helped me get back on my feet again."

"There's no need to thank me yet, Daniel. We both feel that you need another chance in life—everyone does. You are lucky, I guess, but seriously, there's no need to thank us, just start over again. That is more important. I will see you soon," said Dr. Francis.

Dan left with a feeling of hope. He felt like this after a long time. He went through a lot, and it was not over just yet. Knowing that there is still a chance to move on makes a human being feel secure. Dan had the same feeling. Dan reached home without any sign of stress in his mind. He lay on his couch. He saw the picture of his daughters and his wife. Now, his only regret was that his family had left him. He tried to protect his family in all possible ways. Still, he lied to them all along the route to protect them, and when the time came, the relationship broke down, and it was out in the open—destroying the very base of any relationship…the only thing which keeps two people together— *trust.* He thought that once he got a new job, he would try to win them back. He had a feeling that it was his moral duty to serve again in any possible manner. He thought of Diana Francis and Lieutenant Colonel Peter Hawk, who helped him regain his confidence and stand up on his feet. If these two people were not there in his life, he would have shot himself way before this even began. The following day, he went straight to St. James Episcopal Church in New London, now one of the oldest places to pray. He prayed after many years since his second deployment in Iraq. People forget God, but God never fails. He is always there in countless forms. It is just that human beings have to be receptive enough to acknowledge His presence. He confessed about the Haditha massacre to the Father…everything. He asked for forgiveness and the courage to start over again. Daniel was a relieved man now and was ready to face anything that could be thrown at him.

The court-martial date was finalized and Daniel was summoned for one last time. He had already read and signed the agreement. His senior's approval was missing only. Daniel was convicted as per the plea agreement of dereliction of duty and his rank was already reduced to Private from Staff Sergeant. His salary was reduced significantly. Lieutenant General Wisbender approved the plea agreement. Daniel's name was called. He marched in, followed the process, and saluted the General. One of the officers read out the dropped charges and repeated the same lines which Daniel knew by heart. He was issued the official certificate of discharge/separation form DD214 which was received from the military.

Daniel was entitled to government benefits and would be getting some pension as he was not discharged dishonorably. He recalled all the events that led him there, but he chose to think about New York instead, as something better awaited. That was what he felt in the final moments of his court-martial. He got up and saluted the General with his honor and pride. Wisbender got up and moved out of the room. Daniel did not notice Lieutenant Colonel Peter Hawk's presence near him. As soon as he saw him, he greeted him with a salute.

"Let us take a walk," said Peter.

Daniel and Peter moved out of the room. Peter said, "I was observing the whole procedure. You did good, Daniel. Now I hope you have considered Francis's proposal."

Daniel closed his eyes, broke down, and said after a while, "Yes, Sir. I have. I don't know how to thank you."

Peter did not say anything for a minute. Finally, he said, "This is honorable Daniel. You must thank this great institute and not me. It has saved you, not me. This country still cares for those who served this great nation. It still gives you a chance to bounce back. Not everyone gets the same chance. Look at Shepard and Jeremy. Their fates are not the same as yours. Life didn't give them a second chance. Have you paid attention to them? They are miserable. Anyway, now is not the time to crib and regret the past. It's time to move on with life again. Good Luck, Daniel! I hope you serve your country again in some other form."

Peter started moving toward his chamber. He still had many responsibilities to carry out. Daniel was there for a while and looked up toward the flag of the US, which was fluttering in the wind. He stared at the flag for a few minutes straight and then saluted the flag. His heart was filled with gratitude and love for his country—especially the Corps. He did such a horrible act. However, the punishment he received was nothing compared to it. He walked toward his home. He called his father on his way home. He thought that he should finally call his father to tell him about the whole event. While driving back home, he called his father. After a few seconds, Daniel's father, Mr. Dylan Ryan, picked up the phone. "Dad," spoke Daniel.

No voice was heard. Dan repeated, "Dad, are you there?"

After a pause, Mr. Dylan replied, "Why have you called me, Dan? Why now?"

"Dad, I have been discharged from the military."

"This was bound to happen, Son. Why did you lie to us the whole time? Linda told me everything. We are utterly disappointed with your irresponsible behavior. We all knew this would not end well."

'It isn't that bad, Dad. I haven't been dishonorably discharged from the service. It's still honorable, Dad. All the allegations have been dropped. I'm not a murderer, Dad…," said Daniel softly, expecting some sort of understanding from his father.

"It's good for you. We are not a part of it since the day you lied to us, Son. I don't know if the reasons or what you did were right or wrong, but it destroyed your family. Call me when you have successfully redeemed your honor back. The military must have spared your actions, but we haven't. Goodbye, Dan!"

He hung up the phone without listening to his son's testimony. Dan just kept the phone down and focused on his driving. He knew it would take much time to regain their trust. He was looking forward to New York. He decided that he would permanently shift to New York City. Now, only his divorce was pending. He thought he would sell his current home and give his family the entire sum of money, whether they asked for it or not. He wanted them to be financially stable and secure. He did not need money, but they did, and he thought that he would do everything possible to at least secure their future. There was still some time left for the separation procedure to begin, so in the meantime, he thought of listing his house for sale in a real estate broking agency. Dan did all his formalities for the sale auction. His bags were packed, and he was ready to move to New York with only one thing on his mind—how to serve his country again to the best of his ability! He knew the military must have forgiven him to a certain extent, but not the Iraqi people who witnessed the terrorizing event in 2005. He knew he could not bring back the dead, but he would never let any other innocent life get lost as collateral damage. He was also full of gratitude toward God. He thought that once he was settled in New York, he would do anything to bring back his daughters who had left him. He knew it would not be easy, but Dan was not ready to give up on them, though he thought he deserved this separation only to make things right. He was very hopeful for the future. He was gradually making himself ready to start his journey without the Marine Corp following him this time. He headed back to

New York City to find a place to stay, start over and continue with his therapy. He had shortlisted a few neighborhoods near the hospital to rent a small apartment. He spoke to the brokers and started visiting the apartments.

After seeing at least three to four service apartments, Dan realized that he would not be able to afford such a luxury in his life as it was in New York City, one of the most expensive cities in the US. He hesitantly said to the broker, "Can I get something reasonable? I'm not here to enjoy views and lifestyles. I'm here to start over again. Please find someplace which is not as luxurious as these high-end flats."

The broker kept quiet and said, "These were the most basic ones. The high-end ones are not in this area. Anyway, I know a place that might suit your requirement. Come with me."

Dan followed him. They headed toward Brooklyn, where Dan could find an affordable living. The broker took him to a very densely populated Muslim neighborhood. Dan was not expecting anything of this sort. He saw the people staring at him from their balconies. He went back to his past—in Haditha. The faces of these people were so familiar. He thought he was transported back to Haditha. The woman across the balcony was almost identical to the woman spared in Iraq. Their dressing sense reminded Dan of the Iraqi citizens. The children playing football outside reminded him of the lives he took. He was sweating at an almost cool temperature as the place had the same ambiance and surroundings, which made him anxious. He stood there for a few seconds and realized it was not Iraq. It was New York, and those people were not staring at him. His unconscious mind had played a nasty trick with his conscious mind. After a few seconds, he said to the broker, "This place is too damn crowded. I need some breathing space."

The broker observed Dan closely and responded, "At least look at the place first, then decide. There is no hurry."

Dan eventually agreed and followed him into an apartment. He was still feeling unsettled in this place. He was about to enter the flat and thought he was entering one of the houses in Haditha to encounter the insurgents. He tried to remain calm. He experienced flashbacks, and they felt natural to him. Dan thought he was entering the same room where he fired shots randomly, but it was not that room. "This is liveable, Mr. Daniel. Just look at the view outside," said the broker bringing him back to the present.

Dan thought that he had to leave all his memories behind, or else he would not be able to get his daughters back together. The broker said, "This isn't bad for 600 bucks. I could sense that you felt claustrophobic before coming up, but this is not the case here. It's calm and cozy."

Dan thought about how the broker could quickly feel his uneasiness and observed the whole flat from every corner. It had two rooms and a living room. He believed that the broker was right. It was not bad for 600 dollars. He looked all over the place carefully, imagining how he would place everything correctly, and after that, he looked out the main window. He could see a distant view of the Brooklyn bridge. He thought in his mind, *not bad*. The broker said, "This place is not far from your workplace."

He was doing his bit to close the deal immediately. Dan said, "I'm okay with the place."

The broker said, "Perfect! Just deposit the amount in this account, and you are all set to go."

Dan took note of the account details and moved toward the hospital. As per Dr. Francis's deal, Dan would be appointed as a security officer at the New York-Presbyterian Lower Manhattan Hospital. Dan deposited the amount in the landlord's account and started his shifting process. He was carrying temporary pieces of luggage as he never thought that he would take all his final possessions simultaneously. He felt that he would bring all the necessary belongings once he settled in the new city. After finalizing his new temporary home, he thought of visiting Patricia. He looked online and booked an appointment with Dr. Patricia Bell the next day. He reached her clinic in Brooklyn the next day, which was a few blocks from his apartment. The receptionist took down his details and asked him to wait. Dan was reading articles framed on the surrounding walls. He did not pay enough attention to mental health previously, but now he thought that Diana and Peter would not always be there with him. It would be better to talk to a professional for his betterment. After reading almost all the nearby quotes and information, he thought mental health was not a joke. "Mr. Daniel," the receptionist called out and grabbed Dan's attention. He said, "The doctor will see you."

Dan got up from his chair and moved toward the cabin. He was in desperate need of this session. He saw the doctor was not in her seat. Instead, she was busy writing down some notes on her marker board. Daniel did not say anything. He thought of waiting and letting her initiate the conversation. She took her sweet time and then turned toward Dan. She saw him standing as though he was summoned. "Oh, I'm so sorry. Please sit down. I was just finishing my findings on a client. Please sit down. It is not your officer's cabin, so please be comfortable."

Dan sat down and was expressionless. She was very young for a therapist. It seemed like she had just graduated from college. She might have been in her late twenties, probably. Dan thought to himself, *would she be able to understand the gravity of the whole situation?* She was a fair lady with light brown medium-length hair. She looked similar to Linda—as she used to look in their college days. Dan was observing her closely, with doubts creeping into his mind about whether she would be able to understand his problem. *Could I tell her exactly what had happened?* These questions started bothering him before the actual therapy even began. She said, "First of all, I'm sorry you had to wait. Dr. Neil has already briefed me about your current situation. I was expecting you."

Daniel was thankful that she was briefed beforehand. It would be more manageable now. She was so cheerful and calm that it made Daniel a little comfortable. She said, "Daniel, take a deep breath and relax. This is not a drill. Just sit here as you sit on your couch at home. Don't be afraid. This is the first step."

Daniel felt a bit more comfortable. "Now spill out everything nicely and slowly, in whichever manner you deem fit, but please do not hide anything from me. Please, it's a humble request," she said.

Dan took a deep breath and said calmly, "There are two things, Doctor..."

"It's Patricia, Daniel. I'm not your doctor. I'm your therapist. Not only am I a therapist but also a friend firstly, and everything comes next."

Daniel smiled and said, "You can call me Dan."

"Better, much better. Dan. So, let's begin your storytelling journey."

Dan smiled again and said, "So it all started back in Iraq...my second deployment in 2005...all was going well in my life. I served in Afghanistan before Iraq. The situation was different during the Iraq war. Unlike Afghanistan, Iraq was a developed nation. The terrain in Afghanistan was difficult. I was reporting to Captain Shepard, who hated Muslims initially. He made us, all of us, believe that those people are evil-minded. They hated Americans. He made sure that everyone under his command was on the same page. According to his philosophy, Muslims were the reason behind the destruction of peace. After serving in Afghanistan, it was clear that these people were barbaric. But, Afghans are different sects of people, and the Iraqis are an entirely different race of people. Our main target was Saddam Hussein. The Iraqi people witnessed many cruel and brutal acts of dictatorship during his regime, which was a fact. We went there to free these people from his tyranny but what happened was not part of the plan. There were two sets of people in Iraq—one who supported Saddam and one who didn't. Between these two, we were caught up. It became tough for us to identify our real enemy. On one side was the Iraqi military, and on the another, a small bunch of local terrorist groups, including members of Al-Qaeda. They were the hardest to recognize as they blended with the local people and were far more dangerous than the regular military. They killed a lot of Marines in IED blasts. They became aggressive in their way of attacking people once Saddam was captured. We had to counter in response. The rebel groups still disputed our intel. After seeing many of my previous unit's friends killed by these cowards, I decided I wouldn't let any of my men die from an IED attack. I would teach them a lesson if we got attacked by any insurgents in the upcoming days. And so, it happened. We were hit, and Hill was killed instantly. His body parts were scattered all over the road. This enraged me, and I saw those five Iraqis sitting inside a sedan car. They watched everything. I thought they triggered the bomb, ordered them to step out of the car, made them stand in a line, and asked them to confirm that they triggered it. I think they didn't understand what I said to them, and I shot them one by one, trying to avenge my dead marine. This rage did not end there. I took charge of the whole situation and ordered my unit to follow me to raid the house nearby as I heard gunshot shots fired from there. The feeling of revenge and rage also blinded my unit. They agreed to follow me. No one stopped me, and we went inside the house. But we saw no one. I ordered my fellow Marines to find and shoot them. Also, to ensure that no one survives. They did exactly what I had ordered. I searched for them to see if they were hiding anywhere, but unfortunately, I saw a few of them hiding near the closet and under the beds. I just shot them without thinking twice. After executing, I realized that they were small children and women, but I didn't stop there. I saw my Marines doing the same. Evans was urinating on one of the dead bodies of an Iraqi man— the son of a bitch was recording it. It didn't infuriate me at that moment, but now I don't feel the same. I regret my decision every day—during each moment. I lost my family, job—everything. I think I deserved it. I encounter those faces every day. I'm a cold-blooded murderer. I'm guilty and responsible for the whole act, but I'm not happy about it. I think I won't be able to bring them back, but I won't let innocent lives die again. Linda has left me with my daughters. I have no one left, but I will bring them back one day at any cost—whatever it takes. I have disappointed them. I lied to them from the beginning. How could I tell them all this? I tried taking my life more than once."

Dan broke down after recalling the biggest nightmare again and again. Patricia gave him a handkerchief to wipe his tears. She said, "You did good, Dan! I'm proud of you…how you expressed it…all of it…It takes effort to reveal such a dark moment. It is now clear that you were not lying at all. Now, just relax. There are a few more things left that we will talk about but not now—probably next week. In the meantime, I want you to think it was your past and that it doesn't exist. Your future also doesn't exist...it is only now. There is nothing to fear...about something that doesn't exist. There is no need to suffer and lament—for what happened years ago and no need to worry about the future. The existential reality is far bigger than your psychological reality. The fundamental lesson for today is that you can't undo life, but you can learn something from one of the darkest events in your life. Never let your compulsive behavior be a deciding factor for any decision. The biggest religion in this world is humanity, and anxiety is the biggest fear in this life."

Dan was listening to each word very carefully. He thought she seemed far more experienced than she looked. She spoke like a sage. Dan felt that he was carrying a load of this world on his shoulders all along. It was now dropping gradually with each passing day, and he felt much more at ease. He smiled. Patricia said, "Just come down next week and write down if you reencounter the same feelings. Whenever you have these memories again, note down the number of times you do. I will see you again. Good luck."

Dan got up. His body language had changed a lot. He had a particular calm persona. He left for his new home. Patricia's final evaluation report was critical before joining the hospital.

Chapter 6

Manhattan Life

Dan slept in peace, without even thinking of Haditha. All he had in mind was to start all over again. He kept telling himself that it was not too late. He felt that he could still serve his country but in a much better way. He never thought that he would stay in New York, but he had begun his new journey. He thought *it was not a bad start but a good start*. Maybe God wanted him to stand again, and He might just forgive him for his past. He felt that his scars were healed—just a little. For the next few days, he observed that the people in his locality were mainly Muslims from different parts of the world. Many refugees came from Iraq and settled there. The US engaged in war with Iraq for almost eight years—ironically allowed Iraqis to settle down on their soil. They had a refugee policy under the US Refugee Admissions Program, which allowed citizens from Iraq in—after carefully assessing the application. He thought that maybe God wanted him to serve those people this time. He was back to living with those people whom he once imagined to be his country's worst enemies. He remembered how he used to address them—thinking of them as primarily insurgents trying to kill the US Marines. Now he had to live among them. He watched them daily. They had an unmistakable resemblance with the people back in Haditha. Their faces were very identical, and they almost had the same dressing sense. He saw the young, enthusiastic kids playing football in a common area. He thought of starting to interact with them first. The kids who were engrossed in their game did not pay any attention to the man standing right in front of them. "Do you have space for one more?" asked Dan.

The kids had stopped playing and looked at Dan with a curious look. "Do you guys know English?" he asked.

After a pause, a kid said, "This is America, isn't it?"

Dan thought, *of course, they do*. Before Dan entered the scene, they were speaking Arabic. Dan thought and felt that they might not prefer interacting with people outside their community. Dan was about to leave when he observed the football heading toward him. "Show us what you can do," he said.

Dan smiled and asked, "What are your names?"

The kid replied, "I'm Hamid, and this is Zubair. We are running the show now."

Dan liked these kids, and he started the game. For Dan, football was not a thing, but he knew how to play, and within a few minutes, he showed the kids that he could play. Hamid said, "Hmm…You can play a little. You can join us. We play every day at almost the same time."

Dan smiled and replied, "Aye aye, Captain."

Dan enjoyed this session. He knew he would have new friends and a new life. Dan was not interested in thinking about Iraq anymore. He was more interested in starting his new job. The week passed without any signs of trouble for Dan. He thought of talking to Patricia. He felt that he was a little cured of his past and ready to enter the real world, which had been missing for many years. Dan booked an appointment for the next day. His flat was tiny, but Dan had adapted very quickly. He had already started to like it, although he initially disliked the idea of living in the neighborhood. He had started playing football with these kids, which was a good activity for him. The parents of these children did observe this and were quite okay with their children playing with a non-Arab. They were not in Iraq—this was America, and they never imagined that they would have a place in the American heartland. They had already given up their past, and so did Daniel. It was all going fine.

Dan visited Patricia's clinic. He was waiting for his chance. He went through the newspaper's headlines and read about Syria being under attack. He thought of another Iraq in the making. Again, people will die, and another Haditha will occur. He thought that *it had to stop. How many innocent lives will be sacrificed in the name of freedom?* He knew Syria would also face the same outcome as Iraq did in the past. It was Assad's time at present. "Mr. Daniel …The doctor will see you now," said the receptionist.

Dan forgot about Syria. It was time for a crucial evaluation of his new job. Many things were at stake. He could lose that opportunity. He entered and greeted his young therapist. "How are you doing, Daniel?" asked Patricia.

"Good, actually great," replied Dan.

Patricia observed his calmness. She said, "Are you getting proper sleep? Are you able to sleep?"

Dan smiled and said, "Patricia, I'm having a good time with these kids in my building. They keep me occupied most of the evening, and I think we like each other's company. And yeah, I never really paid attention to Iraq, though I'm mostly living amongst Iraqis. Somehow, I don't want to recall Haditha. I just want to start my work now. The only puzzle in my mind is how to get my family here."

Patricia was happy to see her client coping so well. She said, "I'm thrilled that you are doing fine, Daniel. My only concern here is that you are in a rush to start so quickly, which might affect your decision-making. As far as your family situation is concerned, things will manifest in your mind, and then they might turn into a reality. But overall, you are in a good state of mind—well-synchronized with life. Just go slow—not too slow, but at an optimum level. Otherwise, things won't manifest the way you want them. As far as your job is concerned, I suggest that you should not worry about that. It's taken care of. Now just relax. I don't want you to take hasty decisions anymore. Think, evaluate and then act. Don't act first and then think. Remember one thing—the most important of all things, is *choice.* What the world throws at you may not be in your hands, but whatever you make out of it is yours. This is the power of choice, Daniel. So, choose wisely and you are good to go. Enter the world with a smile. Please, never choose misery over pleasantness. Good luck!"

Dan was counseled well. He was ready to face the world again, but this time with a smile.

"Thanks a lot, Patricia. I feel grateful. We need more people like you in the world, especially in the military force, where they teach us how to kill and defend simultaneously, but what happens afterward is not discussed. It creates a scar that finds an expression in the form of depression, stress, and frustration. I wish I had met you and Diana before the incident, which took away everything from me, but that didn't happen. So, there's no point talking about it, but I'm thrilled and ready to move on with my life. Thanks, Patricia and goodbye," said Daniel with gratitude and nothing else.

He got up and left for his new home with a ray of hope, and he missed playing football.

Dan checked his mailbox in the next few days and found two critical emails. The first one was from the New York-Presbyterian Lower Manhattan Hospital. He was excited, but he controlled it. He thought, first, he would go through the whole content and then react. It was mentioned that the organization was happy to offer him the post of ***Senior Security officer***, and he was given a choice to accept or reject it. He calmly read the terms and conditions. After taking a deep breath, he ***got*** the job and smiled, while looking at the window where the sun was shining brightly. He forgot to read the second mail. He thought of celebrating with his neighbors and junior companions downstairs after receiving the notification. After sharing the information about his new job, the people living in his vicinity were thrilled to hear about the nature of his work. He was pleased after a long time and did the right thing. After his gaming session, he thought about the second email from his new lawyer. He knew what it would be about. After freshening up, he sat at his desk and opened his laptop to review the emails. After opening his mailbox, he received another email for his job confirmation. He was allotted a date of joining. He thought two weeks would be enough time to deal with him. Now it was time to read what Hendrik proposed. He opened the email, and of course, it was about his upcoming divorce.

His new lawyer, James, whom he appointed as per a suggestion from Peter, was in charge of the dismissal of the court marital case proceedings. He had emailed the terms and conditions of Linda's lawyer. He was none other than Hendrik. Before reacting, he took a deep breath and thought of just reading the draft first and then responding. His reaction had caused immense damage already. He wouldn't allow his mind to behave compulsively again. He opened the PDF file attached to the email. He read the complete draft and found two significant points of interest.

The first thing was to hand over his children's custody to his wife Linda, and the second thing, the alimony amount was quite huge, but he did not react. He thought, of course, she needed the money to secure her future. The amount was 100,000 dollars. He remembered that he had listed his house for sale which would probably get him 200,000 dollars or more. He thought about the alimony money and agreed upon it but disagreed with the first condition. After considering this idea, he did not accept the agreement and replied to the email that was ready for a few terms and conditions. Still, he was not prepared to surrender his children's custody to his wife. Dan felt that he was doing the right thing after a long time. He thought he would pay double the alimony but not surrender his children's custody to her. He had already made up his mind. He conveyed the same thing to James. He thought that he would have to rent a more convenient place in that block or somewhere else to accommodate his daughters.

The day came after nearly a decade of tragic events. Daniel did wear a uniform but not the one that he was accustomed to—it was a new one. It was not a soldier's uniform, but it was still a uniform. He wore his uniform, which was completely black. He still had a duty toward his new organization, and this uniform still meant that he still had to serve people somehow. He locked his apartment building and went downstairs toward the main entrance. The little kids reacted, "Whoa, damn Dan! Are you a police officer now?"

Dan laughed. "No, kid. I'm just a security guy in a hospital."

"But you look like an officer, man, you do. Do you have guns and stuff?" said Zubair.

Dan replied, "I will catch up with you in the evening—be prepared to lose."

"We will see about that," said Zubair, and his parents smiled at Daniel.

He felt the same way once again as he wore the Marine uniform. Dan walked toward his new reporting place. He had to report to Mr. Shawn, the head of the security of the entire facility. The security staff at the main entrance gate welcomed him, and Dan liked that feeling. He gave the letter and greeted him before entering. He said, "You are on time. He is expecting you. Please proceed."

He pointed toward Mr. Shawn's cabin, which was on the lower ground floor. Dan moved toward the room and knocked. "Come in," said a loud voice that was heard from inside.

Dan entered the room. It was a small cabin full of monitors through which the whole video surveillance could be watched. A guy was close-monitoring all the footage for any foul play.

"You must be Daniel…Please have a seat," said a man.

He was a dark man with a humongous and solid build. He was wearing a suit. Dan sat quietly. "So, you were in the Marine corps. Excellent! I know all about you," he said.

Dan was surprised as he had prepared an introductory speech and rehearsed it. Dan asked, "How? Are you a veteran, Sir?"

"Yes, I am. You have guessed it all right, boy. I took my retirement from the navy a few years ago. I had seen enough. I wanted to settle down in one place. Anyway, how do you like New York?" he asked.

"Sir, it's a great city indeed. I'm trying to adjust, but I will," replied Dan.

Shawn said, "There are a few things that you should know before starting. First, you have to detect any suspicious activity in your surroundings. There are some mischievous and notorious criminals crawling all over space. Second, you must report it. Finally, you will prevent it after assessing the risk. This is how things work here. Effective communication is the key here. I hope I'm clear enough. Any questions, boy?" he asked.

Dan replied, "No, Sir," just like he used to address his superior.

Shawn liked this gesture. He smiled and said, "Go talk to Simon. He will give you the necessary equipment, and good luck with your job."

Dan moved out of his chamber and walked toward the next chamber to meet Mr. Simon. It was just next to Shawn's room. Dan knocked. He could see Mr. Simon from the glass area. He signaled him to come inside. "Daniel, I'm sure Shawn has briefed you. We have a highly military-grade level of communication set up here."

Dan found it to be amusing, but he controlled it. "Get all your equipment from there," he said.

He guided him toward a walkie-talkie and some cables lying at the next desk. "Gear up and start your patrolling. Come—come on," he said.

Dan took his new equipment, and there was a list of radio channels for various areas. He was ready but also curious about why there were no guns. He observed that all the security personnel did not have arms. He hesitatingly asked Simon, "Simon, do we have firearms here?"

Simon got irritated as he went through some crucial emails and said, "Guns! Do you want guns in a hospital? If you wanted to fire guns, you should have joined the army or police force. This is not the place of firing arms. This is where people fight between life and death, and you want guns!"

Dan quickly realized his mistake, apologized, and said, "I'm sorry, I was stupid. Wrong question. My bad. I should go."

Simon said, "Don't worry about it. Just focus on work."

Dan left for his duty and thought, *what was I even thinking asking for guns?* At the same time, he laughed about Simon's remark—that he should have joined the army. He began his duty by observing the hospital. After a glimpse of that place, he thought it would be a mess, as people created a ruckus for trivial issues but thought it was the same in the army. Focus, patience, and communication were the three pillars that he always worked upon to succeed in his military career. He thought he would implement the same here. He thought the situation there could also get complicated. Many doctors had to maintain calm as patients and visitors created panic, and security had to be called upon to tackle such problems. Dan thought about why even security would be a concern in such a medical facility. Soon after spending just a few hours on his first date, he knew it would not be as easy as he had imagined. He observed a young man who screamed at the top of his voice. He was in pain. He met with an accident a few days ago and needed medical care. Nurses and even a few doctors tried to calm his relatives down, but the situation got a little out of hand.

Dan put channel five on his radio to report any unusual activity. He said, "Sir, first-floor emergency ward—a few people are getting out of control. Permission to intervene."

"Noted, Daniel. Proceed."

Dan, like a soldier, walked toward the severely injured young man. He looked at the man and said, "Sir, please calm down. We are here to help."

The patient could not respond. Dan asked his relatives to be quiet and asked the nurse, "What is the problem?"

She said, "Just take him up and get him to the physiatrist at rehabilitation. These idiots think that by performing surgery, he will be fine."

"Roger Ma'am," said Dan as he called out for a wheelchair.

After making him sit in the wheelchair comfortably, he started moving toward rehab. Dan did not say anything as he took him away.

After the rally, he saw a man wearing a lab coat and working on a computer. As soon as he saw Dan with a patient, he immediately said, "I will handle it from here. Stevan, come here now. I haven't seen you around."

Dan handed over the patient. He instructed his junior to take him inside. His assistant, Stevan, came and took him away. Dan said, "Yes, Doctor, I just joined. This is my first day, and I think this is what I must do."

"Oh, so the first day. Welcome to Presbyterian."

Daniel was looking at the whole rehabilitation center.

"My Name is Thomas O'Brien. I'm a physiatrist. This is not a regular hospital. It's more of an educational hospital, but we have more than 150 beds for patients, and yeah, of course, we have a rehabilitation facility for these injured patients."

"Sorry, Doctor, but what is a physiatrist?" asked Dan curiously.

Thomas laughed and said, "I'm a physician, and I have a specialization in medicine and rehabilitation. It's not just a fancy word."

Dan acknowledged it and said, "I'm sorry, Doctor, you have much responsibility on your shoulders. Good to talk to you. See you around."

"See you, Dan. Good day!"

Dan left for his duty around the hospital. As his shift was over, he thought it was time to play with his little footballers. He left for his home, feeling delighted that it was not bad. He never thought that he would be able to get back to his usual self. He picked up groceries on his way home. As he was getting his stuff packed, the news flashed about how the Syrian President, Assad, used a chemical gas, *Sarin,* as a bio-weapon on his people and killed thousands of Syrians a few months ago. The US and NATO were trying to impose various sanctions on Syria and its allies for using biological weapons on their people. Again, he thought those geopolitical wars would not stop, and only innocent people would die—no matter which side one belonged to at that time.

It was the same agenda, different nation—that shit would remain the same. He thought that there was indeed another Daniel Ryan who was getting ready to face the harsh reality of warfare. "Damn these politicians and dictators," said Daniel in disgust.

Everyone around him noticed his reaction. He thought again, *what do I have to do with it?* I should focus on building up my life again. "Sorry," said Dan taking his stuff and moving toward his block, which was not far from the departmental store. As soon as he entered his building, he saw that the kids were busy playing football. He said, "Now, don't you guys start without me. I will be there in a minute."

"Come fast," yelled the boys.

Dan smiled and started walking fast. He did not want to lose his playtime. He reached his apartment, put his stuff in the living room, changed quickly, and ran downstairs. He was happy. After the game was over, he prepared his dinner for the night. He switched on the TV and news about Syria was everywhere. He wondered about what he could do—nothing—just observe the information. Dan gradually started his new life and enjoyed his new lifestyle where there was plenty of time. He never thought he would get so much time in his lifetime. As he finished his dinner, he thought of checking his mailbox. As expected, James had replied about the divorce case. He opened the mail and mentioned that Hendrik and his client were not ready to hand over the custody of the children. He got frustrated, decided to speak to Hendrik directly, calmed himself down, and planned to talk to James first. There was no point in reacting and making a mess of that situation. He took out his cell phone and called James, who had been handling his cases since court-martial. "Hi, James. How's it going?"

"It's about time you called. I expected you to call me earlier," said James on the other line.

"Sorry, James. I got stuck with my new work."

James interrupted him, "Oh, sorry! I forgot to ask, how is New York, man?"

"It is awesome. I like it here better than in New London."

"That's great to know, man. Good to hear this, but now let me come directly to the point. That son of a bitch, Hendrik, won't let you get the custody so easily. I'm guessing you might have to pay two hundred thousand dollars. Then, I might be able to crack this deal down. That bastard knows you are entitled to government benefits and you have listed your house for sale—though he doesn't know where you are and what are you doing. Now tell me, Dan, what do you want? Do you want to settle this down once and for all? Do you want to drag this out for a while? Your choice."

Dan thought there was only one way left to get his daughters back—for which he had to pay considerable compensation. Dan thought, stood for a while and said, "James, you get the papers ready. I will get the money arranged sooner or later—this has to end. I can't do this any further. It's about my daughters' future. I can't lie back and accept it. Just try to get this deal cracked for me, buddy—two hundred thousand for my daughters. I'm ready for it. Please get it done, James. I am counting on you."

"All right, Dan. That is a wise decision as nothing is left between you and Linda. Sorry about that, but I'm on it. I will update you soon regarding this. You just get the money ready. The sooner we have it, the better the chances of a bargain. Let's see what happens. Good night, Dan," said James.

"Good night," he said.

He hung up. Dan thought Linda was having an affair but ignored it as it would not work anyway. He wanted to secure his daughters' future and give them a new place to start over—just like he had given her a chance in life. Now he rechecked his mail, especially the spam folder, to see if the broker had any listings regarding some offers. Indeed, there was an offer and the broker had given his contact details. He noted his number and decided to call him the next day to get the deal done.

Chapter 7

Paying the Dues

Dan slept quietly, thinking about his daughters and what arrangements he would have to make in his apartment. His main priority was to sell the house as soon as possible and the only way was to crackdown a deal with the broker. He called up the broker the next day to get the deal done somehow. The broker told him that a buyer was interested in his property but would charge about eight percent commission of the total amount promised in the deed, eight to ten percent for the court, and other formalities were separate. After thinking for a while, Dan said, "get me two hundred thousand—the rest is all yours, but I won't settle for less."

The broker said, "Fine, just give me a few days. I will get back to you."

Dan liked his new job, but his daughters' custody and the final settlement were the only things that made him feel concerned. He often thought, *would they like New York? This was a tiny apartment compared to the old house.* These questions started bothering him. He had just begun his new journey, but he knew he had won the biggest fight, which was the court-martial. While on a regular day at work, he received a call from a real estate broker. He informed Daniel that the deal could be made. His client was ready to pay Dan's required amount.

Dan said, "Okay, just tell me when to reach New London to finalize the deal. I will have to apply for the leave."

The broker informed him that he had to reach out to complete the deal's formality by the following week. Dan said that he would be reaching New London by the following week. "Just get this deal done for me. It's really important for me."

The broker said, "Consider it done."

Dan felt relieved. At least he could pay the required amount to get his daughters back eventually and return his stuff to New York. He thought that it was probably too early to ask for leave as it had been just a month at work, but he felt that he had to leave for new London. He would make sure that he got a casual leave approved by Shawn. He thought that he would inform Shawn about the urgency to go for a few days. He explained his family situation. Shaw was convinced and approved his leave application. Dan was pleased with the organization. He immediately called James to update him about his sudden visit and said, "Hey James, I will be there next week. The house deal has almost been finalized. Of course, you will be the attorney for that. I will be ready to pay the demanded amount…"

James interrupted him in between. "Dan, listen…Sorry to interrupt, but I have convinced Hendrik that we are willing to double the amount for the custody of the children. Now he is asking for proof of income… he needs to know how you'll be able to manage the expenses of the daughters. He needs proof of income stability…of your bank account statements and stuff like that. I will work on your house deal. It's not a big deal. One of my juniors can manage and handle that."

Dan said, "That could be arranged."

"Don't worry about the income proof. I'll share the documents with you soon. You will have them. Just be prepared on both fronts."

"All right, Dan, awaiting the docs. See you."

Dan knew that he had to share them one day, so he had already sorted out the documents. His new updated bank records were awaiting. The next day, he sent all the documents to James. The documents were enough to justify that Dan had almost the same income in the military or slightly more than what he was entitled to which included various government benefits. He earned more than he used to as a Marine in the US army. He had a good and steady source of income. He was confident that he would be able to take care of his daughters in a far better way than Linda. He called James and explained the same facts. He said, "James, now that you have all the facts, let us just finish this. They will have the required amount as alimony, and the court can't deny me custody of Elizabeth and Jessica."

Dan was desperate to get this thing off his mind as soon as possible. He also told James to talk it out with Hendrik and get a date the following week. "I want to return here with my daughters," he said.

James understood his desperation, and he could understand his urgency to finish the deal. James said, "I will try my best to get the deal done by next week only because you have mutual consent. They also need the money at the earliest…focus on the sale. Without it, nothing is moving forward. We don't have much time. As soon the deal is agreed upon, I will get it notarized, and we are good to move forward."

"I'm already on it," said Daniel.

Next week, as per plan, Daniel left for New London and was hopeful of getting his family situation sorted out completely. The broker had given him hope, and so did James. He reached his old town in just a matter of a few hours. He had already packed his main stuff before leaving for New York. He had to sort out his remaining stuff and transport it all to New York. He had booked a pickup truck from a transport carrier company. He thought that if he could finalize his divorce, he would shift his stuff. The broker called him and said, "It all looks good, Mr. Daniel. We just need to complete some formalities on paper, and the fund will be transferred into your account minus my commission, of course. You have to move your stuff out quickly. My client wants to move in immediately, like before the holiday season."

Dan replied, "I'm already on it. Just transfer the money and get the papers signed today. I don't have much time."

"All right, I will get it done now."

The broker thought Mr. Daniel was in a tremendous hurry to close the deal—much more than he was interested.

While packing his remaining luggage, he thought of calling James and asking for an update. He called him up. "Hey James, I'm here. What's up with Hendrik?"

"Good to hear from you, Dan. Things are going as per plan. I think your financial documents have shut them down, and it worked. Man, they thought you must be working hard to meet your ends. Your new job has worked in your favor, buddy. Get the money transferred as soon as possible and I will deposit it in the court. They are out of options now. I guess. Get to the New London Superior Court on Thursday, and after that, we will get the custody from Child Services as per the court's order."

Dan was glad to hear such words from his lawyer—that what he intended was happening as per plan. He signed the papers, and all the formalities were almost done. He thought of calling his father and telling him about what was happening. He called him without hesitation. He picked up the call and said, "Dan, where you have been? I heard that you are selling our house. Is that true?"

"Yes, Dad, it's true…I don't have any choice…I'm doing it for my children—their future," said Dan.

"Okay, I understand, Son, but what about you? Where have you been for months? I didn't hear from you since the court-martial. What have you been up to, Son?" asked Dylan curiously.

"Dad, I have shifted to New York. I have a job here in Presbyterian Hospital as a security officer, and it isn't bad, Dad. I have something to fall back upon," replied Dan, who felt a little emotional.

"That is great, Son. You couldn't have asked for more in life. How did you get this job, Son? I mean, I'm happy for you. When can I see you, Son?"

Both of them got emotional. "Today, Dad…I will be there today… we will have dinner together."

The broker handed over the agreement papers, and Dan forwarded the soft copy to James to get it legalized and adequately formatted. James texted him back—*all looked good. I think Thursday is your day. You will come out victorious in both situations.*

Dan felt relieved knowing that, finally, things were moving forward systematically. Dan left for his father's home in New Haven, which was far from Dan's house. It was an hour's journey by public transport. He took the evening train and reached the old house where he lived during his childhood. He always admired and wanted to join the military, just like his father. Everything went on perfectly until the Haditha incident took place. He had left all that behind to focus on his present. He reached his destination on time. He was greeted by his father, who was eagerly waiting for his arrival. They were indeed happy to see each other after a long time. Dan tried to control himself. He was trying not to cry. Dylan said, "Let us prepare our supper."

Dan smiled and helped him prepare the food. "What is going on with Linda?" asked Dylan quietly.

"I think the court will decide in the next few days," said Daniel.

"I know you both are getting divorced, but what about my grandchildren?" asked Dylan.

"For the same purpose, I'm here in Connecticut, Dad. Everything revolves around money. She needs two hundred thousand dollars and then she will hand over the custody of your grandchildren to me. I had to sell the house though you guys bought it. I will take them to New York, and I would request you to please be at the house for the same purpose on Christmas," said Dan.

His father did not say anything. Dylan said, "How did you manage to get yourself out of the mess and secure this sort of a job?"

Dan said, "There were people from the military who helped me out...and..."

"I knew it...they would help. They would never leave any fellow soldier behind. This is the US. You should be proud of it," said Dylan interrupting in between.

"Yes, they have. I will always be grateful to this nation. I still have to serve them in any manner possible," said Dan with a sense of gratitude.

"Your mother would have been proud of you…Stay here tonight."

Dan nodded his head. He cleaned the dishes and went to his old room. He saw his childhood pictures. He broke down, remembering his mother, who had passed away many years ago.

The next morning, Dan was about to leave for New London. Dylan said, "I will come to New York. Just take care of my granddaughters."

This boosted Dan—he got approval from his father. They hugged each other. Dan could not control his tears this time. As he left for New London, James called him. "Both the drafts are ready. Just sign them and the rest will be done. I got in touch with the broker. He will hand over the draft to me. The rest of the formalities are almost done."

"Perfect…thanks a lot, James. You have worked hard for me, buddy."

"Don't worry about it, Dan…I want to see you and your children live your lives to the fullest rather than remaining in the past and be half a step in starting over…sign them today at my office. Bye," said James.

Finally, Dan transported all his belonging to New York and his wife's possessions from their previous home to James's office. He went to his office and signed all the papers. He read them carefully as he was used to reading a lot during the trial. James's assistant said, "All done, Sir."

Dan got up and said, "Thanks."

He called the broker and said, "The keys and everything are at James's office. Get them picked."

"All right, Mr. Ryan, the deal is complete now. All the best," said the broker.

"Thanks."

Dan returned to have a glimpse of his old house for the last time. The following day was crucial as he was waiting to see his daughters and take them to New York.

The day came. It was time. Dan spent his last day in an almost empty house, dressed formally to appear before the court. He called James. "Is everything ready?" asked Dan.

"Yes, Dan, we are waiting for you," said James on the other line.

"I'm almost there, James, it'll hardly take a few minutes."

He booked an Uber to New London Superior Court. Dan was now familiar with trials. He did not bother much about the court. He was just a little scared of how his daughters would react. James was standing outside the building and waiting for him. "There you are…about time, let us go."

Dan did not have time to react. James said "Let us just go through the final draft. Thank God for the timed negotiations with Hendrik which were fruitful. Otherwise, the dates could take up to a year for the first date of the trial."

Dan said, "That is why Peter recommended you, buddy."

James pointed out toward the corner, "Watch out for Hendrik. He is watching you." "Let him watch. He can't do anything now, but where are my children, man?" asked Dan.

"Don't worry. As soon as you both sign the draft in front of the judge, he will order child services for custody—they will be here soon," replied James confidently.

They both waited until the hearing was called for and the moment came. Dan got a little nervous about how he would face Linda again. They both entered the room where she met the Judicial officer who was sitting in front of her. Behind her was Hendrik, who was just giving Dan and James a weird look. They both ignored Hendrik and took their respective seats.

Linda did not even bother looking at Dan. She was not interested in any sort of conversation. Dan noticed rudeness in the whole room. He also remained silent. The officer read out the final draft with every term and condition. There was silence in that room—as if it was a church's confession room. He asked if there were any objections. Both said "no" simultaneously, as if they both wanted to get rid of each other very badly. He gave them a file and told them to sign it. Linda was the first to sign it, and after that, Dan did. The officer said, "The final order will be handed over by this evening. The attorneys can collect it. You are free to go."

Linda just got up and left, and Hendrik followed. "I don't know whether to congratulate or sympathize with you. Let us just get your daughters and then you may leave," said James.

Dan just nodded his head. He thought, *just look at the audacity of that woman!* After taking so much money, she did not give a damn about anything. He got up and the moment of reuniting with his daughters arrived. James took the court's order to hand over the custody to their father. They came out of the building. Linda and Hendrik were probably gone. Dan saw his daughters waiting outside the court's main entrance. Dan just ran toward them, and so did they. "Daddy," screamed both of them and they grabbed their father.

Dan saw them after almost a year now. He thought about what Linda must have told them, which would have made them upset, but during their reunion, it did not seem to be that way. "How are my angels? Look at you! You've grown up," said Daniel.

"Where were you, Dad? Mom said you left home and the army had thrown you out."

Dan did not react the way he used to before responding. He said, "No dear, that is not true. I live in New York now, and so will you now. Daddy works in a hospital. Don't worry about anything. Daddy is here now, come on, get your stuff. We are leaving this city."

The girls were fascinated once they listened to the word *New York*. Dan turned toward James, and without saying anything, he hugged him. Dan said emotionally, "You have been like my guardian angel, James. When there was nothing left for me, you and Peter stood by me and without you both, I wouldn't have been standing here."

James smiled and said, "This is my job, Dan. I help my clients."

"Come on, book a cab now, go. It is about time to start over again," said James.

Dan smiled, took out his cell phone, and booked an Uber to New York. He said, "Thanks a lot, buddy. Whenever you come to New York, I'm just a call away. Please hand over the remaining things that are lying at your office to Hendrik."

"I will surely do that. Good luck, Dan," said James and he walked toward the court.

The cab arrived after a few minutes and they all left for New York. Dan thought it was about time not to look behind anymore and just look forward.

Chapter 8

The Misguided Youth

They reached New York in about four hours. Liz and Jess were too engrossed in just looking at the beauty of New York City. The Statue of Liberty could be seen at a distance. They both told each other that it was just like in the movies. Dan was just watching them and he smiled. He thought that he would have to take a bigger place now, though the flat could accommodate them after arriving from New London. It was tiny, but he was out of options for now. They reached Dan's block. They both thought it might be a big apartment just like it was shown in the movies, but they were about to get disappointed. It was a very crowded neighborhood. The driver left. Dan took out the luggage and told them to move with him. "Dad, what is this place? It is filthy. How can you live here?" asked Jessica, who was not accustomed to such a place.

Dan kept quiet and moved toward his flat. As soon as they saw so many Muslims, they were terrified and said, "Dad, are you sure you live here? I think we are in the wrong place," repeated Jessica.

Dan did not get furious. He said, "Just help me."

They finally reached the flat's door. Dan opened it and they all entered. Their reaction was the same as Dan's first *not bad* glance. "See, I told you it is not that bad," said Dan.

"When did you say anything about good or bad, Dad?" Jessica asked.

Dan realized that he did not say a word about the place. They roamed here and there—it was a decent place, but nothing more than that. Dan showed them their new room—the biggest room in the flat. "Come on girls, this is your room. Unpack your stuff and I will be there in a moment."

Dan went downstairs to breathe fresh air and saw his old friends playing football. Zubair said, "Look who is back."

Dan smiled and did not say anything. "Will you play or not? And are they your daughters? You never told us that you were married and had kids."

Dan said, "Not today, Zubair."

They continued with their game. Dan was concerned about how they would adjust and their admission to a new school. Those questions made him worried for a bit and he suddenly saw this strange young guy standing in a corner with his crutches and watching the football. Dan never saw him around, so he called, "Zubair, come here," out of curiosity.

Zubair said, "Oh, come on! First, you don't play, now you call me in between."

Dan asked, "Who is this new guy?"

Zubair looked around. "Who, where?"

"That one, you dumb kid," Dan said pointing toward the direction where the tall guy was standing.

"Oh him, I don't know his name. He came from Syria, I think. His family lives on the third floor. He came the day after you left. He doesn't speak much and is always lost in his world, and yeah, he watches football very closely. That's it now, let me play."

He had grown a long beard with long hair. From his initial impression, he looked scary. Dan observed him and thought that the war might have made him that way. He thought about Thomas and that he would be able to help this guy. As he was going upstairs to his flat, one of the women who interacted with him asked, "Are those your daughters?"

Dan did not know her name and said, "Yes, it's a new place for them."

The woman said, "Let them be the way they want to be. Tell them to interact with us and they will feel better. I know what American kids think of us, so it's better to start early to change their perception."

Dan understood the gravity of the situation. She knew that they would not be comfortable there. Dan said, "Indeed, you are right, their perspective plays a vital role, especially at such a young age. I will make sure that they don't fall for this trap. Thanks for your cooperation. Do you know this lad who is standing and staring at the game? I haven't seen him around…"

The woman said, "Husam, his name is Husam. He came from Syria. It's a mess now. Some Syrian refugee family has adopted him in the building. I think something nasty happened to him, just like a thousand others in Syria."

"I work at Presbyterian Hospital—in the security department. If he or anybody needs any help…just to let you know…I'm there for all of you." said Dan.

The woman appreciated the gesture and said, "That is kind of you. I will surely let you know. He needs medical assistance."

Dan went to his flat and saw that his daughters were preoccupied with watching TV. He said, "Do you want hamburgers?"

They screamed "Yes!"

Dan took them to the nearest eating joint. As they were having their dinner, Elizabeth asked, "Dad, what happened in the army?"

Dan knew that they wanted answers, so he said, "People died in my command, and I had to pay the price for that. So, they gave me a choice to either serve in the army with a feeling of guilt and shame or to serve people respectably by leaving the army. I chose the latter."

"But Dad, Mom told us that you killed innocent people! Did you?" asked Elizabeth while Jessica was enjoying her burger.

Dan thought Linda did play her last trick by briefing them. "Yes, Liz, when the enemies are disguised, it's tough to understand who the target is, and sometimes we shoot the wrong people and they die."

Liz did not understand what her father was saying. As per Linda's briefing, Dan would not be able to answer such questions, but he did, which made Liz run out of options regarding what she should ask now. Dan's priority was to manage their admission into their new school somehow.

The following day, he got ready and was about to leave for his job. Before leaving, he prepared breakfast. As he went downstairs, he saw that boy in the same spot. He was motionless. Dan thought he would talk to Thomas about him that day. The Arabian woman appeared in front of Dan. She was a typical Arabian woman. She wore the usual Arabian clothes and had light green eyes and a beautiful face. She said, "Please help him. He needs a wheelchair and has no parents. I'm the only one he has got. My name is Nafisa, and at no stage, can I buy him that now. I heard you can offer help."

Dan understood the pain and suffering of the guy and said, "Don't worry, I will take him to Presbyterian very soon."

Dan left for work. He now had two priorities. It was a regular day at work. He went to Thomas and requested that he treat a patient. Thomas agreed and told him to bring him to the rehabilitation center. It was his job to take care of people. Dan was glad about the response and thought he would pay for his expenses. The next thing in his mind was school. During lunch, he asked his colleagues, "Which is the best high school, like affordable, in Manhattan?"

After a short discussion with his staff members, Simon said, "Stuyvesant—it's a good option. Research about it and talk to the management."

Dan said, "Thanks, Simon. I will."

Dan reached home and found his daughters watching YouTube with Zubair and other children. He was happy. He never thought it would ever happen, but it did happen quickly. He thought about talking to the new guy again at the same spot. He approached him and said, "Why don't you also hang out with the rest of them?"

He did not respond as he did not listen to what Dan had said to him. Dan said, "I know your name is Husam, right? Are you alright?"

He was quiet for a few moments and said, "You might know my name but you don't know anything about me."

"I may not know anything about you, but I will be taking you to Presbyterian."

Husam said, "What is that? A mental asylum?"

Dan thought he had been through a lot, judging by the rudeness with which he was answering. "No, it's a hospital. They will run diagnostics for your leg and give you proper treatment," said Dan.

"And who would bear the expenses?" asked Husam.

"I will," replied Dan.

"May I know the reason for this generosity?" asked Husam.

"Just trying to help, nothing else," replied Dan, surprised by the counter questions from Husam.

He did not reply. Dan assumed that it was a *yes*. "What's your name?" asked Husam.

"I'm Daniel Ryan, but you can call me Dan. Hey, listen, I'm just trying to help. I will send in an ambulance tomorrow. See you around."

He did not respond. Dan thought it was a good chat. At present, he had to figure something out about the school. As soon as he had some time, he searched for information on the school. He emailed the management and forwarded the necessary details to the concerned person. Little did he think his ex-military career would help in this organization as well.

The next morning, he sent an ambulance to pick up Husam. He reached Presbyterian hospital, and Husam was taken to the rehabilitation center for evaluation in a wheelchair. Dan was waiting for him at the entrance and talking to Thomas. Husam was just 20 years of age, but he looked like he was in his late 30s. He saw Dan wearing a security uniform and said, "From Marine Corps to a Security guy."

Dan felt a little weird and angry at the same time but did not say anything. "You are ex-military, aren't you?" asked Husam again.

Dan said, "Yes, I was."

"Because of people like you, I'm here," said Husam.

Dan got a little irritated but did not react. He thought that maybe Husam was in trauma just like he was a few months back. "What happened to you…I mean, how did you end up here like this?" asked Dan very calmly.

"I told you, because of you people—you don't let us live."

Dan thought maybe it was too early to ask those questions. Thomas intervened and said, "Come on, Stevan, take him inside."

Stevan took him inside, where Thomas would start the diagnosis. Thomas said, "The guy must have faced many difficulties and tragic events. Anyway, I will run my diagnosis and let you know very soon."

Dan replied, "Thanks, Thomas and I don't think he will be able to bear the expenses so, I will bear the cost."

Thomas said, "Daniel, I think you would get it adjusted from your wages. These bills will cost a minimal amount to the employees."

Dan said, "Oh, that would be great! Let me know once you are done."

Thomas went inside, and Dan also went toward the security room. Dan came to enquire about Husam later in the evening. He saw Thomas sitting in his chamber and knocked on the door. Thomas called him to go inside. Dan said, "How did it go?" Thomas said, "Both of his legs are amputated. It is like something sharp slashed his legs and most importantly, he is under much stress. The stress can be seen on his face. He is just 20 years old as per his ID, but he looks like someone around my age. He needs a psychological evaluation."

Dan listened carefully. Later he said, "I will get him a wheelchair for now. At least it is better than using crutches."

"Don't worry about it, Dan. It's free from the hospital's side. It's the least we can do."

"Thanks, Thomas, that would help him a lot. Can I take him home now?"

"Yeah, sure, but do take him to a therapist soon," said Thomas.

"Yes, I will," replied Dan.

Dan immediately thought of Patricia. Stevan made him sit in his wheelchair and Dan came and said, "I'll take it from here. Thanks, Stevan."

Dan took Husam toward the apartment. It was a half an hour walk back to the block. "Why are you helping me?" asked Husam.

"I'm not. We live in the same building, so, that is why I'm taking you there," replied Dan.

"I'm not talking about that. I'm talking about helping me ease my pain," said Husam.

"I just want to you walk once again," replied Dan. Husam said," I know who you are, Staff Sergeant Daniel Ryan. You have killed so many innocent people back in Haditha, I know everything…"

"No, you don't, Son, only I know what is the truth—what happened back there. The Internet only gives you a brief overview—a small fragment of the truth while the real incident is completely hidden from the mainstream audience. Anyway, I left the Marine Corps more than a year ago."

Husam was not expecting this sort of reply from him. Now it was Dan's turn to ask questions. "I think you know something about me. Now, mind telling me what happened to you? How did you end up in such a way?"

Husam replied, "Do you know anything about Ghouta?"

Dan thought for a while and then he said, "Honestly, no."

"Then you need to search about it and you will figure it out yourself."

Dan kept quiet. They reached the apartment. Dan was surprised to see Nafisa waiting for him. They thought it was too late. She was so delighted to see Husam in a wheelchair. Nafisa said, "Thank you, Sir, for your help. I don't know how to thank you. We have lost everything. We don't have anything to give you in return."

She started crying. Dan could feel the pain. He said, "Please don't thank me. It is my job, and it's the least I can do for you. Sorry for your loss back in Syria."

Dan handed Husam over to her and went upstairs. He saw Nafisa's smile, which was priceless. Dan thought he did the right thing that day. Dan was a little curious to know about *Ghouta* and what it was about. Dan searched for it and found it during Syrian civil war—where the chemical attack occurred in Ghouta in August 2013. He read about how the Syrian President used the nerve gas, *Sarin* against its people and killed thousands of them. Husam was probably a victim of this attack and must have suffered immensely. These tragic events must have made him the way he was right then, which must be horrific for him as it was for those who had suffered in Syria. He saw videos in which the people who were exposed to the gas were choking and fainting. Dan's empathy had grown not just for Husam but for those who had suffered during wars. He could now feel the pain of those Iraqi people whose lives Dan and his company had taken out of a sheer mistake. Dan presently thought that the Haditha event was an accident and he regretted his decision. He checked his email and found a notification from Stuyvesant High School which stated that his children's application was approved and the interview date was mentioned. Dan was relieved that the application was not rejected and told his daughters, "The interview is on the 24th. Come on, girls, start your preparation."

Liz said, "I don't want to go to school. I like it here."

"Oh, so you don't want to study now…interesting. You didn't like this place at first. What happened now?" asked Dan.

"It is quite fun here, actually."

Dan smiled and said, "Come on now you two, it is important. I want you to get the best education possible."

All of them smiled and went out for dinner. Dan had forgotten that he had to look for a new place and so did his daughters. He never expected that there would be life after the court-martial, but there was, surprisingly. He was doing something which was least expected of him. Life changes and people should also change accordingly. Otherwise, life will find ways to change you. It might look harsh initially, but it is for your good.

Dan's empathy toward Husam had grown a lot. He thought of inquiring about Husam from Nafisa and know-how was he doing. He asked, "Is he a little better now?"

Nafisa replied, "I don't know what he is up to. Most of the time, he just sits with his laptop. I don't know what he searches for all day."

Dan listened and replied, "You should talk to him."

"You think I don't try? He is so obsessed with this internet thing that he is not bothered about anything else. He doesn't step out, and I'm not his real sister. I don't even know who his birth parents were, I knew him from the Zaatari camp. He was with me. He was very close to Nadia, but the terrorists killed her right before his eyes. Our name was on the list of refugees who were allowed by the Americans to enter, and we left Syria heartbroken. I took pity on him after her death and decided that he was my brother from that day onwards. I promised him that I would take care of him and now he doesn't listen to me. Just make him understand that he needs to resume college or take up a job or something. Please, you are all we have in this strange city," said Nafisa.

Dan replied, "Please don't worry about him. I will do all that is within my capacity. Please bring him. I will take him for his treatment."

"Thank you, Sir. We will always remain indebted to you," said Nafisa.

Dan said, "Please don't call me Sir. I'm Daniel. You can call me Dan."

She smiled at him. She grew fond of him. She brought him on the wheelchair which was far better than those crutches. Dan carried him toward the hospital. He was quiet—as usual. Dan broke the silence and said, "What do you watch on your laptop?"

Husam did not say anything. "I asked you a question," repeated Dan.

"I watch videos of how America is always eager to provide freedom to the other nations by attacking them—killing thousands—just for what? Oil?"

Dan thought he did ask a genuine question, and it was his moral right to know.

Husam further asked Daniel, "What went on in Haditha?"

Now it was Dan's turn to remain silent. After an awkward silence, Dan said, "It was an accident. It's in the past now. I remember it as a tragedy and I was responsible, no question about that."

"Do you feel guilty about it?" asked Husam.

"Each day, I wish I could somehow undo the event but I can't, you can't—the past is only powerful till you want to carry it with you. The day you decide it doesn't exist, it has no power left to affect you, it does exist but only in your *memory*, not anywhere else. But I won't let anyone go through this type of trauma again," said Dan.

"So, this is why you are so kind toward me. Where was this kindness when you and your team brutally assaulted those children and women with your bare hands?"

Dan was a bit scared, knowing the intensity of Husam's way of asking the question. It was not like he was asked this question for the first time, but it was a chilling experience for him. He answered, saying, "It was war. I didn't start it. War is between one man's versus another man's beliefs. We are puppets, being played with by either. I lost many brothers in Iraq and swore that no one would die in my command, but it didn't work as per my plan. Someone died right before my eyes. I could have died there. I had to protect the rest of my team, so I did what I had to, but it turned out to be a massacre. I'm not lying. It cost me a lot. I'm still trying to repay it. Trust me, I didn't want to kill anyone. I still remember those faces very clearly and I know you must have searched for me on the internet. I don't deny anything, so this is all of it, and yes, I'm doing it for myself, not you."

Husam was a young boy who had faced a lot in his life before coming to New York. He did understand Dan's perspective a little. At least he was not lying. However, he did not say anything. It was the school's interview date, so Dan dropped Husam at the rehab center and went for the interview. He went back, picked up his daughters, and booked a cab. The question asked by Husam still occupied Dan's mind. The school's interview went well. Dan was not expecting any relief with the fee structure, but being an ex-military helped him get their revised design for his daughters. He was relieved because Dan would otherwise not be able to afford the school fees. Elizabeth and Jessica were blown away looking at the school's campus. It was far better than their previous school. Dan thought all was going way better than it was expected. His only concern was Husam and his questions. He thought *I will ask Husam how he landed up in such a condition.* Dan asked his daughters, "Did you like your new school?"

"Yes, Dad, it is amazing! I loved it," said Liz.

"And you Jess?"

"It looks better. Let us see how the studying experience is," said Jess.

"Fair enough," said Dan agreeing with Jess, who was younger than Liz but more mature regarding knowing what was good and bad. Dan dropped them at the house. The school's classes were to begin the following week, so they did have time to play. Dan returned to work and after a few hours, he talked to Thomas about Husam's condition. Thomas said, "We need to perform amputation surgery, which is risky and costly."

Dan asked, "Will he be able to walk again?"

Thomas replied, "I would suggest just getting one leg treated. By doing this, he will be able to walk a little, but he can't get off the wheelchair completely, and he doesn't have insurance. I guess you would have to pay for it. The best I could do is reduce the cost. Even then you would have to pay 25,000 dollars. You decide."

Dan thought that it was way too expensive but thought he could withdraw that amount from the savings which were left for his daughters' school fees and reduce it significantly. "Go ahead with it, Thomas. I will pay for it," said Dan.

Thomas said, "You are doing him a great favor. He would be grateful to you forever."

Dan replied, "I want him to be hopeful in life, not grateful to anyone."

Stevan brought Husam back to him. Then Dan carried him back home. On the way back to the building, Dan said, "I did a little bit of digging on Ghouta. I can't imagine being exposed to nerve gas. It's the worst form of an attack against your people and I'm sorry for you."

Husam just had this wicked smile on his face and he said, "Oh don't feel sorry for Ghouta. It was a hoax and an isolated event and trust me, there was never a gas attack. It was just chlorine gas which made us go crazy for a while. But it was presented in such a cinematic fashion to the world that it seemed big, while the real picture never surfaced. This is sort of the world we live in, Mr. Ryan."

Dan was stunned by the reply. He was not expecting that reply. He wanted to know more, so he asked, "What do you mean by that? I mean, the whole international media covered that story."

"Mr. Ryan, people only see what the media wants them to know. That doesn't mean that it must be true."

Dan was speechless for a few seconds and asked, "What happened to your leg Husam?"

"Now you are asking the right question. This happened because of shelling. A car exploded before me—taking away my legs."

Dan froze and remembered a similar situation where Hill died from an IED explosion in Humvee. Dan did not have the guts to ask him anything further. Husam was not finished just yet. He was just getting started. "Don't you want to know how I ended up here?" asked Husam.

Dan said, "Oh, sorry, I just remembered something similar. Yes, I do want to know. Please continue."

"Some other time, Mr. Ryan. We are almost home. Thank you for your help. The doctor said that you are willing to pay my medical bills."

Dan said, "Yes, Husam, I know you have suffered a lot, but all I'm doing is nothing compared to what you must have been through back in Syria. I'm not helping out of compassion. I feel I must serve as many people in need as possible—that is it."

Husam remained silent. Dan returned to his flat, where his daughters were busy watching TV. His mind was stuck in Husam's past. He thought about how hard it must have been for him to cope without his legs and in such challenging situations. This made him believe even firmly that he was doing the right thing to help him reduce his pain. As Dan was busy thinking of Husam's condition, Nafisa was happy to hear that Dan was ready to pay for Husam's surgery. She hugged Husam. He was also pleased because he had met someone who genuinely wanted him to help. Nafisa thought, *let me thank Daniel for his valuable help.* She knocked at Dan's flat's door. Both of Dan's daughters were preoccupied with YouTube. Dan knew they would not open the door. He went to open the door, and as he opened it, he was surprised to see Nafisa at his doorstep. Nafisa said, "Thank you for your help," and hugged Dan.

Dan was not expecting this as he had not hugged someone in a while. He had no chance to share his love with anyone else in a long time. They both felt the warmth in each other's arms. They both shared a kiss that came unexpectedly in the most uncalled-for environment.

Chapter 9

The Cyber Warfare

Jessica and Elizabeth were not the only ones who were busy on the internet. Husam was also busy browsing the internet. He was not watching the videos that he told Dan about. He used the *dark web browser*, where the IP address cannot be traced back. He was trained to use the internet as a weapon to find targets that could get training virtually and act when the time was right. To find the proper contender, Husam used to upload Abu Bakr al-Baghdadi's video on various forums on the dark web daily. Abu Bakr al-Baghdadi was the leader of the most wanted terrorist organization in the world. He was a commander in the Al-Qaeda group before its name changed to ISIS and later, he became the leader.

Husam could not fight on the ground level, so he received special training under which the internet was used as a weapon. He was steadfast in his belief. He was brainwashed so that the only thing he was focusing on was finding a suitable person to carry out the acts of terror. He was not getting the desired response, which made him frustrated. The video that he used to post online was handed over to him by his organization itself. The content of the videos was nothing but motivational techniques where the Holy Quran was interpreted in such a way that the person became rigid and narrow-minded. This was the classical technique used by most terrorist groups to radicalize their point of view. It was an effective way to brainwash young children, and in case someone had suffered in war, this worked wonders as they sought revenge for their wrongdoings. The same was the case with Husam. He had suffered a lot back in Syria, where the civil war broke out due to much international political intervention and which resulted in havoc in Syria, in the same manner where war broke out a few years ago in Iraq. However, he was getting some responses from people who were afraid of getting caught. Husam needed someone who could sacrifice his life for the cause. While he was getting help from Daniel, his real motive was his mission to cause something like 9/11. The basis of his training was 9/11, as it was used as a success story of organizations such as Al-Qaeda and ISIS.

Dan and the people living in the entire block could not have imagined that someone in their building was planning something so big. On the one hand, Dan was full of empathy and love for Husam and Nafisa. On the other hand, Husam was busy searching for a target. Finally, the day came when Husam's mission had found a contender. As usual, Dan carried him to the hospital. While on the way, Dan asked him, "You should complete the story."

Husam did not understand the question. He said, "What story?"

Dan asked, "You have to tell me how you landed here in the US."

"Oh yeah, I remember. After the attack on Ghouta, I never saw my parents again. My whole family was wiped out. I don't know whether they are alive or not. After some causal treatment, I was thrown into the Zaatari refugee camp like other living Syrians.

I always loved football, but it was taken away from me. It was the only thing I had ever loved. I spent a few years in the camp. I think your government had pity on us and decided to allow some refugees into their homeland. It is a nice gimmick. First, you attack us and show the world that you are doing some charity and care. That's the ironical part," said Husam.

Dan had no words to tell him. He was now sure that he was doing the wise thing. The surgery went well. His amputated legs were replaced with prosthetic limbs and he was way better at walking, even with crutches.

Though the phantom limb pain was not entirely gone, still, he was a little better—to carry on with his life. The wheelchair was an added accessory for him. Nafisa was full of gratitude toward Daniel and had fallen for him. Dan, on the other hand, also grew fonder of her. She thanked Daniel for his efforts and contribution. Dan said, "I would help in the best way possible."

Dan's heart was full of joy—as if he had found someone comforting and loving again in the unlikeliest place with an unknown woman who was not even from America. They used to go for walks together. It was all about sharing and caring for them.

Husam was discharged after a week. He also did thank Dan, but he thought of dropping his mission for a moment. But the motivation was so strong that he could not resist it. The feeling of revenge is far more robust in terms of manifestation than the feeling of forgiveness. His heart was full of gratitude toward Daniel's efforts. He thought he had made mistakes in his life, but he was a wise man at present, so why should he be the same way? He thought of dropping his terrible idea, but his mind was not ready to accept that idea so quickly. He had to take revenge for thousands of brothers and sisters, and Allah was on his side. That was why he was getting aid to complete the mission. Indeed, there was a battle—an inner conflict, searching for a reason, and he did not know which side to choose. Dan asked Thomas, "Does he still needs counseling or therapy?"

Thomas replied, "It's hard to say, man. Initially, he needed one, but he is slightly better. I would rather say, I don't know. You do spend too much time with him. What do you think?"

"I need to ask him more questions first. Thanks, Thomas. Please thank the surgeon and his team from my side."

"I will, Dan, see you around."

While they both were leaving, Dan asked, "How are you feeling, Husam?"

Husam said, "Much better, thanks to you. Listen, I will pay back your money. I don't like donations, Mr. Ryan."

Dan asked sarcastically, "But for that, you need to earn, buddy. I heard you are always busy on your computer. What do you want to do?

I might be able to help, you know. Think about it and tell me whatever you decide."

Husam thought Nafisa was giving away too much information to Dan. She could prove to be a danger to his mission, so he decided to be more careful. He had an idea that they were close now.

Dan asked him again. "So, what have you decided? You also haven't told me what you plan to do next."

Husam also replied sarcastically, "If I told you about my next step, you would not carry me in the same as you pushing me right now."

Of course, Dan did not understand the full reference, but he got an idea—he was up to something. He randomly asked Husam, "Are you planning to plant a bomb near the Empire States building?"

Husam was taken aback. He had forgotten that he was a Marine before, and messing around with him might prove to be fatal for his plans. So, to cover it up, he said, "That won't solve the world's problems. It will only exasperate more problems. I plan to get a job somehow and I would love some job at the New York football club."

"Interesting. Now you are talking in the right direction. Let me see what I can do, and please remove these thoughts from your head—the destructive ones. I can sense revenge pretty damn easily."

Husam was now scared. He thought he had just messed with the wrong guy. Now he got a hint—he remembered his training and the art of manipulation. He thought, *no more silly mistakes.* He had to act smartly and focus on the mission.

After handing over Husam to Nafisa, Dan said to her, "Meet me as soon as you are free."

She got a bit scared as Dan looked suspicious of something. They met up for a usual walk. Nafisa asked, "Is everything all right? You looked worried about something."

Dan replied, "I'm not worried—just doubting that Husam might do something stupid. I see some form of rage in him. I know this feeling very well. I had the same feeling once and I paid the price. I want you to keep an eye on him without alerting him."

Nafisa was scared and had a worried expression. She used to get tensed now and then. She held Dan's hand and said, "I think he is still not over Nadia's death. He had changed once she passed away. Okay, don't worry. I will do whatever you say. Just don't leave me."

Dan knew she was a highly emotional lady, so he did what he had to. He hugged her and said, "Hey, I'm not going anywhere. I'm just worried about him."

Dan was working hard in life to set things right this time—for his daughters, Nafisa and Husam. Finally, after months of struggles and waiting, Husam found a guy who was inspired by Abu Bakr al-Baghdadi's words.

He asked Husam on a private chat (he remained anonymous on the dark web), "The things they have done to our people will not go unnoticed. Tell me, what can I do?"

Husam thought it was time to tap into the situation. Husam replied, "If you want to go to heaven, you have to do something big for our people and Allah. What is your name?"

"I am Umar. I want to prove my worth to this holy organization and show that we are not alone. We can also fight. This country treats us like crap. They kill us at their own will. It's time they should also take us seriously."

Husam thought he had finally found the guy whom he had been seeking for many months. Even though he was not ready, he had shown the necessary will to execute the mission. Husam asked, "What do you do?"

Umar replied, "I'm a driver. You just give me an order. I will run these Americans over."

"Hmm, that is a good approach, Umar, but where do you live?" he asked.

"New Jersey," replied Umar.

"That is not far away from New York. Listen carefully. We need to be tactful. Things have changed since 9/11. We have to think practically. Firstly, the motive should be clear. They have to pay for their wrongdoings. Secondly, the impact should be devastating so that they will never forget ISIS," said Husam.

"Why only New York City?" asked Umar.

"Because it is their heart. Our allies chose the Twin Towers for the attack to maximize the message's magnitude. They still have not forgotten the 2001 attack. We have to do something similar. They consecutively attacked us in Afghanistan, Iraq, and Syria. They won't stop until they fear us. These people are deaf to your sorrows and blind to our pain. They need a wake-up call—a gentle reminder that we have not forgotten our mission. Remember this—Allah is with us on this mission. He has chosen you for this holy mission. You have to teach these *Kafirs* a lesson. They are against our religion and our mission, kill your people as they wish, rape our women, kill young children, and put us in gas chambers—these people have no right to live. If we don't fight back, they won't stop. You will be the *hero* for many others. We will rise again, and they will fall."

This speech gave Umar a healthy dose of Islamic extremism, which was necessary to carry out such activities. Husam further added, "Come up with at least three plans. I want to check whether are you a worthy candidate for our holy mission."

Umar replied, "Believe me, I'm ready, master. I will share the plan's details soon."

Husam replied, "Come back on the same IP address when you are ready. Not before that."

The conversation ended. Husam finally got a volunteer to carry out the mission—a mission that he was trained for in Syria by non-other than Abu Bakr al-Baghdadi. He knew he could not fight with his hands and feet, so he made a fight sitting in a wheelchair. Husam knew much work had to be done to extract the best out of Umar.

Nafisa did what Dan asked her to do—keep an eye on Husam. But currently, Husam locked himself in his room. He was alert by then and did not give any chances to her. She told Dan, "He locks himself up and never comes out. Something doesn't seem right."

Dan told her to grab hold of his laptop somehow or try to check what he was up to in his room. Jess and Liz got their admission. Dan was pleased to see his daughters get through one of the best schools in New York.

Umar was getting more desperate than Husam to execute the plan, though he did not know what he could do to please God and go to heaven. The extremism did its job. He already hated Americans by then. The idea acted as a catalyst and the reaction would be devastating. All he thought of was to take revenge. He thought he would hire a propane gas truck and blow it up in some crowded area in New York. Then, he thought he didn't have a commercial truck license and he was off contract with his previous employer and could not enter New York without proper permits. He knew it would be a road rage attack, as he knew how to handle every type of vehicle. He contacted Husam using the Tor browser, which was untraceable, but you had to use a strong VPN to stay invisible completely. Still, neither Umar nor Husam used a VPN, which was still traceable by any good hacker. Husam was also eagerly waiting to hear from his prodigy. As the conversation began, Umar said, "I have come up with a plan to hire a truck from a local depot at Passaic and go straight toward New York to start our Mission."

Husam said, "That's it, that is your plan for our holy cause? That is nothing. Listen to me very carefully. Yes, the truck can be used as a weapon for killing many, but you need training for that. Have you ever killed someone by running over them?"

"No, Master."

Umar thought he was dealing with some experienced mentor. He never thought he was taking instructions from a twenty-two-year-old guy sitting in a wheelchair. "Listen carefully now. Go to New York, find the busiest route and plan your timing. Timing will be the key here. Try executing it during the holiday season. That will give a strong message to the *Kafirs*. Tell me something, do you have a family?" asked Husam.

"Yes, Master, I have three children but don't worry about them. I'm only focused on our mission. They are not bigger than our mission. Our religion is in danger. We have to save it or else everything will be finished."

Husam thought that it was damn easy. He just got influenced by Abu Bakr al-Baghdadi's speeches and videos on Islam and the Quran. Husam was proud that he would make ISIS proud and avenge all those who were killed in the Syrian civil war. He said, "Good. You will be Allah's soldier now. Don't get distracted from your mission. Go immediately to New York and start recking now."

"I'm on it, Master," said Umar, who was now thrilled that it was indeed going to be a vehicular attack. The next day he drove to New York not as an Uber driver but as a soldier who came for the reconnaissance of the site. As he entered the city, he parked in the Hudson Street car park to study more about the areas. The only thing in his mind was what the route would be. He thought *I could begin the attack anywhere. Still, that endpoint is important and what is better than the One World Trade Centre building, which was rebuilt after the terrorist attack in 2001?* At least he had decided what would be an endpoint. That building was to be the focal point. He then opened Google maps on his cell phone and searched for One World Trade tower, which was hardly 1.5 km away from where he was standing. He thought that he had found his road map for mass execution. He would start from his parking stop, kill everyone on his way to the One World Trade Centre building, run for the Brooklyn Bridge, and not get caught. He was happy to have found out the route of his mission and was thrilled to share this news with his master. He reached his home back in New Jersey within a few hours. He contacted Husam. Umar said, "Master, I have found the route."

"*Masha Allah*! Share it with me," said Husam.

"I will start from Hudson Street and end at—guess what?" asked Umar.

Husam, who hardly had settled in New York for about six months, did not know what Umar's excitement was all about. He was irritated and said, "You don't ask questions, you answer."

"I'm sorry, Master, I thought you must have guessed it by now. Anyway, I was talking about the One World Trade Centre building and then running toward Brooklyn bridge. That's my plan, Master."

Husam replied, "Excellent, good work. It will send a devastating message to these people and this attack will compel them to listen to us. But you need to learn more about the truck and how many lives it can take. What if you get caught in between? Think about every aspect. No stupid mistakes."

Umar replied, "Yes, Master, I will work on your suggestion for our cause if you can make arrangements for guns."

"You must be capable enough to arrange a few weapons, but good job, Umar. I believe in you, and so does Allah. Just work on a few more things, and we will execute it on Halloween day. It will have the least resistance from the opposing force," said Husam.

Umar agreed and said, "That will be even more wonderful. I will work on these fronts now."

Umar was happy that whatever he had planned got approved and was on the right track. For the next few days, Umar just watched videos of how pickup trucks could run over pedestrians and some related videos on accidents. He had the affirmation that he would be able to kill more than a dozen people that Halloween and even had thought that he would probably escape the crime scene. Meanwhile, Husam contacted Imran, an ISIS leader who had helped Husam get clearance while he was on the Refugee list—which allowed him to enter the US. Husam informed him that Umar was ready to sacrifice himself for the mission. Imran inquired about the proposed plan. Husam explained the entire plan to him. Imran was an experienced militia leader who knew that Umar would get caught in between and there were no chances of escape in that mission. It was a suicide mission. He explained to Husam, "The plan is just okay. There are many things such as how and who will claim responsibility for the event. The execution should be precise. One silly mistake and he who is on it would compromise the mission. Next, train him so that he praises us for our glory and think of a backup plan."

"Yes, *Janab*, I told him to get some weapons. Once he gets caught, he will terrorize more Americans," replied Husam.

"Good, make it happen, *Khuda Hafiz*."

Husam was relieved that his commander was impressed with him. He was sure that he would make himself and the organization proud.

Umar knew that he would not get a weapon so easily, so he thought that he would get paintball as well as pellet guns for backup and tell his master that he had real guns. Now, he had only one thing in his mind— just somehow, he had to execute it as soon as possible. There was at least a month before Halloween. He kept himself busy by watching and searching for ideas about how to run over people. His mind was radicalized enough and he was ready to kill. Meanwhile, Husam thought he would plan more attacks if he was successful in his plan. Little did he know what would happen next. Daniel was busy with his work as he thought everything was settling well for him. His daughters got their admission to one of the best schools in New York. He was earning decently. He contacted someone at New York City football management. As a Gulf country owned it, they would help someone from their region, especially after looking at the condition of Husam. He received a positive response from their side and they asked for Husam's resume. They told Dan that they would probably consider him for some profile. Dan was happy with the response and told them that he would be emailing them soon. Dan met Nafisa and asked whether there was *any lead*. Nafisa said, "None. He is very cautious. Please, I have a bad feeling about this."

Dan said, "Don't worry, I'm trying to sort out a way so that he might get a job and do something with his life. I'm here."

They were both in love already. Dan thought that he would check on Husam personally and tell him about a piece of good news. He reached his block and it was his game time. He saw Husam interacting with others and thought he looked happy. He called Zubair and asked, "How is he doing now?"

He replied, "Man, he knows a thing or two about football. Sadly, he can't play, but he knows the game pretty well."

Dan smiled while looking at the kids. "I'm coming. Wait for me," said Dan and went to change.

After the game, Dan asked Husam, "How are you doing now?"

"Good, thanks to you, Mr. Ryan…just teaching them and giving them some tips about the game," replied Husam.

"I heard that you know a lot about football," stated Dan.

"Not much, just some useful tactics," replied Husam.

"Hey, I have something to share with you. I need your resume," said Dan.

"Resume? For what?" asked Husam.

"You wanted a job, right? Remember? I spoke to someone at your football club. There is a chance, but I can't guarantee you anything," replied Dan.

Husam had lost all his hopes, but this man was just not ready to give up—the same way Nadia was not ready to give up on him. Immediately, he thought of abandoning his mission and concentrating on his new life. He thought that he would delay or probably cancel the mission by making Umar stop. After thinking for a while, he said, "That's wonderful, Mr. Ryan, I don't have one, but I will prepare it and hand it over to you." "Sure, do that. Who knows? You might get lucky," said Dan.

Husam thought *I must speak to Umar today and stop him.* He did not realize that it was too late. Umar was already fully prepared—to execute the mission. Husam already had a confirmation message from Imran that the Halloween mission would be completed. He contacted Umar later that night. Before Husam could undo his initiation, Umar said, "I have got the guns, knives as well as the ISIS slogan and messages. I printed everything just as you had asked. Halloween is not very far away now. Wish me luck, Master. I will make you proud."

Husam thought that he had gone too far, but he still had to try, so he said," Good Umar, you are doing pretty well, but there is a change of plan our superiors have recommended rescheduling the date of the mission immediately. We will hit them on Christmas. It is a much bigger festival and would have more impact than Halloween."

Umar did not understand his master's sudden change. He said, "But Master, I'm fully prepared, and I'm doing what you told me to do. I can't go back to my usual cab-driving days. I was destined for this mission."

Husam did not know how to stop him. He again tried and said, "You can't disobey the order."

Umar disconnected the chat, and before leaving, he said, "I don't think you are my Master. He would have never said anything like that."

Husam knew that he was too late. Umar had been severely brainwashed and now, he could not go back. Husam could only pray that somehow it would not happen. He was just a scared young boy—caught in the wrong front and facing unpleasant situations. He prepared his resume and decided that he would not get back to the past events that had made him the way he was right at that moment. The next day, Husam handed over his resume to Dan, feeling hopeful that he would be able to start over again in life. Later, Dan told Nafisa, "There is nothing to worry about. I think he is on the right track now. I think he is working for his job now."

Nafisa was glad to hear this, but the principle of life is based on cause and effect. You have to bear the consequences of your deeds.

Husam prayed to God, asked for forgiveness, and requested God to stop Umar from carrying out the terror attack. But it did not happen as per Husam's wish. He was the one who planted the seed of vengeance on Umar's head, who was already short-tempered as was evident by his social behavior and conduct. Umar just needed a little push, that is all.

Chapter 10

The New York Attack

On the day of Halloween, 31st October 2017, Umar slept like he usually did the previous night. His family had no idea what he was up to at present. He was waiting for the day to arrive. Everyone was in holiday mode. He rented a pickup truck from Home Depot in Passaic in the afternoon. As per his plan, he reached the Hudson Street parking spot. He was surprised to see fewer people on the street. He had anticipated a large crowd on the road so that it would become more accessible in terms of crushing the people. He did have a second thought about why the Master wanted him to reschedule the attack. He was somehow obsessed with the idea of killing people, clearly indicating that he was already not in a precarious state of mind and now was becoming mentally unstable as well. It was all stored within him from the start—his daily clashes with his customers. All he needed was a little push which he received from Husam. ISIS's brainwashing strategy did the rest. He took a deep breath and started his truck by saying, *"Allah hu Akbar."*

He started his truck and began his rampage by getting started in the bicycle lane and he found many cyclists. It was the perfect opportunity to set fear in the minds of the Americans—that was the thought he had in his mind.

Now all he had to do was pinpoint the truck's steering wheel toward its target—just like a gun, which he learned from watching videos online and what he did in life. He crashed into two cyclists. They never saw something like that coming. Umar ensured that the truck adequately crushed them and he did not stop. Many unfortunate and innocent people were walking, cycling, and crossing the road. Suddenly, a pickup truck destroyed everything on its path. Umar had this sick smile on his face.

He said to himself, it's all so easy. It was as enjoyable as playing a video game that made the protagonist crush people. He enjoyed this madness. He had crashed into more than a dozen people, killing many instantly and losing count. There was a strange silence on the street. People did not realize what they had just witnessed. The real panic began. Umar hit so many people that even the truck was severely damaged. He was not far from his real target, which was the One Trade Center building. He thought *I will just crash my vehicle into the building to maximize the damage and send these Americans a message.* Suddenly, he lost control of the car and it crashed into a school bus that was carrying children at a tremendous speed. That was not part of his plan. He thought it was time to threaten those children and nearby people with guns. He got out of his truck carrying a pistol, was screaming *"Allah Hu Akbar"* and was running around with no thoughts about regret or shame in his mind. He had a long beard and he was fully dressed as a terrorist. He thought he had just avenged so many Muslim lives that were taken in the name of power. He pointed the gun at many youngsters who ran in fear and panic. Suddenly, a gunshot was fired, and Umar was shot in the abdomen by a brave police officer, putting an end to an act of terror. Umar was down but said, "This is just the beginning. There will be more," and laughed while taken into custody.

Husam's prayers were unanswered. He witnessed the whole act on the local TV channel and was devastated. He cursed himself and asked himself why he did not stop Umar initially. He never wanted to do this. He was just a victim himself who was played with by two contrary forces. He was disgusted but thought he would never be caught and would not do any such thing further. He destroyed the pen drive and erased all the ISIS data from his laptop.

Meanwhile, in the New York-Presbyterian Lower Manhattan Hospital, Dan and the staff were also alerted. Dan panicked a little about his daughters as he saw a terrorist hitting the school bus, but he calmed himself down. He radioed Shawn and the others to take positions and be on high alert knowing that the terrorists could attack that hospital.

Shawn agreed with Dan and ordered each member of the security staff to take their positions at the gates and call 911 for backup. Within a few minutes, the police reached the hospital and started securing the perimeter. Dan called Elizabeth, but she did not answer. Dan panicked a little more, but as an ex-marine asked the police officer whether the terrorist was caught or not.

The police officer replied, "He is under custody."

Dan was relieved, and suddenly Shawn radioed everyone to be prepared for an emergency as the victims who were hit by the truck were brought to the hospital. Everyone got ready. The ambulance arrived and the patients were taken into the emergency ward for immediate treatment. A few were declared dead within a few minutes, while others received the necessary treatment. Dan wondered who could have committed such a deadly crime. He saw a glimpse of Umar on the news. He was a young Arabian man with a full-grown beard, carrying a pistol. He saw a few children getting seriously injured on TV. He wished and prayed for his daughters. Their adjoining areas were barricaded and the network was barred. Dan thought, *how could the CIA have missed something that big?* After his shift, he ran toward his house and saw a big traffic jam extending up to many miles. Somehow, he managed to reach home, all the while hoping and praying for his daughters' safety. He saw nobody in the building. He got more anxious. He dashed toward his flat and as he was about to reach his doorstep, he saw Nafisa and his daughters hugging each other while sitting in the corner. They grabbed him and started crying as soon as they saw him standing before them. Dan asked, "How did you guys reach here?"

Liz replied, "The police officers dropped us from school. I saw the killer roaming around the building—smiling even when he was shot. He was terrifying."

Dan calmed his daughters and took them inside. Reassuring them, he said, "It's all over, don't worry, I'm here now."

What was odd in all this was that the people of the building were not to be seen anywhere—as if they all had escaped except for Nafisa.

Dan went outside to look, and suddenly his cell phone rang. It was from a private number. Dan answered the call by saying, "Yeah."

"Hello Daniel," said a familiar voice which was heard after a long time.

Dan recognized it. It was Diana's voice. "Ma'am," said Dan.

"I think our destiny is somehow connected, Dan. First, Israel and now New York. Come outside from your building quietly. We need to talk," said Diana.

"Yes, Ma'am, but my daughters?" asked Dan.

"Don't worry about them. I won't let anything happen to them. The building is surrounded. We have intel that the mastermind of this attack is inside this building. As we talk, we had surrounded the whole area before you arrived, so you didn't see anyone around. They are all inside, awaiting further orders. Come out," said Diana.

Dan reassured Nafisa that he would take care of it and asked her to take care of his daughters in the meantime. Nafisa took them inside.

Dan exited the premises. He thought about the term *Mastermind.* Who was capable enough to plan something of that size? He wished, *please God. Husam is hopefully not the one. They are all mere refugees from the Gulf countries.* Dan reached the main street. He saw two Cadillac SUVs stationed in the corner. An FBI officer asked Dan to follow him. Dan went to the SUV and the FBI guy opened the door. There was no surprise—Diana waited for him.

Dan got inside. He did not know how to react. He was pleased to see his mentor, but at the same time, the situation was not pleasant. Diana said, "Officer Daniel, long time. I was sure we would meet but not like this. Anyway, I will come to the point…we were following a lead. We intercepted a conversation between an ISIS rebel leader and someone carrying out recruitment on their behalf. We have uncovered a conspiracy in which ISIS had trained young boys to racialize people and use minimalistic weapons such as vehicles to attack. It is not just in New York—they have done it worldwide."

Dan was stunned, and his mind kept telling him that somehow it was Husam behind all that had happened. He wished he was wrong. "Ma'am, how can I be of any help to you? Please order," said Dan.

"I know, Daniel. You want to know why you have been called. I know you have been living here for almost a year. You know these people well by now. I'm not saying that they are all culprits, but there is someone very cunning and shrewd. That idiot thinks he is smart enough. By just passing information, he is not so. The dark web isn't secure enough. He wasn't using a VPN and that is how we could track him. Now tell me something, do you have doubts about anyone? It could be anybody," said Diana.

Dan took his time and said, "I'm sorry, Ma'am, but I can't confirm and say for sure whom you are exactly looking for, but there is one guy who might have done something like this. For that, I need to be sure, or else it will be unjust for all these people living here. They have already suffered a lot by our hands directly or indirectly. I don't want them to live their entire lives thinking that they are still looked down upon by us."

"Fair enough, Daniel, I understand your point of view, but due to somebody's action, we have lost many lives today. Listen, if you are not willing to help, I can understand, but we have our way of handling things, which I'm sure none of us wants."

Dan said, "Please check on someone called Husam."

Diana instructed the guy sitting next to Daniel. He replied, "I'm on it."

Dan's wish was not going to come true this time. "Mohammad Husam…interesting…I knew it from the start," said Diana.

Dan curiously asked, "Ma'am, what happened? Please tell me."

"Listen, Dan and listen very carefully…This guy is dangerous…a report claims that he was initiated and trained by Abu Bakr al-Baghdadi himself…we can't say that for sure, but what is interesting is that his name was put on the list by one of the allied ex-agents. That is weird, but it's a fact. Why would Rachel do something like that?"

Dan tried to process all that and asked, "Who is Rachel?"

Diana analyzed the information and said, "She was an MI5 agent who worked with the CIA on the Syrian mission."

"What mission, Ma'am?" asked Daniel.

"That is classified, Officer. All I can tell you is that there is more to this than we know," replied Diana.

The conversation was interrupted by an analyst who said, "I have something on Mohammad Husam…somebody at the Zaatari camp in Jordan had a connection with ISIS. That guy had informed Tariq, the ISIS leader, about Rachel. After Rachel was executed, her laptop was recovered and revealed that she had helped Husam get to the US, not ISIS."

Diana was surprised and silent. She was thinking about something. Dan was not able to understand what was going on. He said, "Ma'am, you have to fill me in."

Diana started narrating the incident, which led to all that had happened.

Chapter 11

The Civil War

(2011, April, Daraa, Syria.)

Since the arrival of the new President, Bashar Al-Assad, Syria started experiencing the use of new technologies, such as mobile cell phones and the internet. Before his succession, nobody in Syria could dream of such a thing. The people living in the country thought it was mere imagination and nothing close to reality. Since the Assad regime took over, the Syrians thought it was about time that their land would also witness growth and development. Bashar al-Assad was thought to be a liberal and development-oriented leader. Who would have thought what destiny had in store for Syria and its people?

However, in Daraa, the Arab Spring movement had picked up its pace as the President of Tunisia Zine El Abidine Ben Ali and Egypt's President, Hosni Mubarak stepped down, making the newly Syrian rule a volatile state, a victim of proxy war and a market open to infiltration and exploitation. The whole rising of the Arab Spring movement was designed to change the regime, and the message could not have been any clearer. A young Syrian boy was getting instruction from a leader to execute his mission. He was told, "This is just the start. You have to be focused and clear in your mind. Syria doesn't need Assad's legacy," said the old spiritual leader of the mosque.

Mohsin replied, "I know what I have to do."

He walked toward his old school to complete his mission. He hardly knew that what he was about to do could trigger a war that would last almost a decade.

(2013, Ghouta, Damascus, Syria.)

Syria had witnessed the horrors of the civil war since the first quarter of 2011, which started from Darra's peaceful protest and turned into a modern proxy war. The Arab Spring movement boosted the neighboring countries, such as Saudi Arabia and Turkey. They wanted to dethrone Assad in the same way in Egypt and Tunisia. The oil-rich nations that had earned billions of dollars started funding anti-Shia propaganda. However, Iran was a close ally of Syria and supported Syria in countering these newly-formed enemies. This move made Turkey plunge into the war with one agenda—the end of the Assad regime. When Syria had Russia's support, it was not easy for enemy forces to completely invade Syria.

Damascus became a battleground and a victim of a westernized idea of a free nation. Syria was rich in natural gas and crude oil—just like any other gulf nation. So, the western nations had eyes stuck on Syria for its natural resources. Modern warfare is an event in which the occurrences that are projected and portrayed are not necessarily actual. The absolute truth is always concealed regarding how the acts of war are executed. That is done so that it cannot be cracked easily unless someone has leaked information about the reality. The international media, which is controlled by powerful nations only projects what is necessary and where their interests lie. The facts remain hidden until some journalists try to uncover the truth, which seems impossible. Syria was such a case. However, many countries in the past became a victim of this strategy. Iraq was one nation that paid heavily for its oil.

The Syrians living in the suburban areas of Damascus, known as Ghouta had become a base for Syrian rebel forces, though the city was not very far from the capital. The Syrians were stuck on both sides of the cities. Ghouta was a stronghold of the newly-formed Syrian rebel forces, funded and trained by the US and Saudi's money with only one thing in mind—to remove Assad somehow. The town, which once flourished as a growing society, now had become a center of operation for rebels.

These mercenaries' main aim and focus were to capture Damascus at any cost.

The millions of people living in Ghouta had tremendous fear in their hearts, as they knew that it would become increasingly ugly and deadly with time. They stayed home, and most people refused to come out during the daytime. Indeed, it was hazardous. Seeing it as an opportunity for recruitment, the rebel leaders deployed soldiers to find anyone who could fight for their cause. They propagated that the only way they could be free was by removing President Assad. They got some success, but not all Syrian mothers would want their young children to die a merciless death. So, many people refused to support that idea. However, many young teenagers had given up already. They used to stay indoors, hoping and praying for the war to get over. Then there were the daring ones who in such a condition even when the whole city was in a mess and curfew. They somehow managed to sneak out with allies and made it to the football pitch in the children's playground. The most entertaining sport for the youngsters living in the area was football. Mohammad Husam was one such enthusiastic teenager who was always excited to play football. He was much taller than the usual kids that were around. He had a pretty long face with light brown eyes. He had so much energy. He always waited for the time when his friends would call him to play. Since the school was not operational due to the ongoing war between the two armies, these youngsters were the happiest compared to anyone else. They never thought that they would get so much playing time. However, Husam's parents were not fond of this idea. His parents always scolded him, but he never listened. His elder sister, Fatima always cared for him and allowed him to sneak out of the house most of the time.

The central part of Damascus city was destroyed due to motor shelling. The effect of war had not fully reached Ghouta yet. The people living in those areas were concerned about their lives because they sensed that they could get hit anytime. They all lived in fear and were afraid of losing their dear ones, as the war was so unpredictable. The local men used to gather around the meeting point and discuss the future of their nation, as they did not choose this war. They were plunged into it forcefully by the West. The war did not decide to pick them. They were just baits—ready to be crushed anytime. It was 21st August 2013. A few days had passed, and there was no sound of gunfire and shelling nearby. The people thought that they could finally get some relief after the havoc unleashed by both ends of the armies. Suddenly, the suburbs of eastern Ghouta started to hear loud noises, and this time, the noise was louder than the usual sound of bombardment. Husam was playing football with his friends in the main street's playground. All the bombs exploded. Everybody in the neighborhood panicked and started running to seek shelter underground. Husam and the boys freaked out, and they all started running toward their houses to check on their families. As they moved closer to their homes, one of the bombs dropped near a car, and it exploded so fiercely that it almost knocked down all the boys who were running across. Husam and his friends were lying unconscious in the streets.

After the shelling stopped, an ambulance searching for survivors in the aftermath found Husam and two of his friends lying in the corner with blood streaming all around the street. They immediately rushed to check them. The support staff checked for a pulse and said, "No pulse."

Two of them were dead on the spot. One had a beating, but his leg was cut off. Husam lost one of his legs. He did not realize it as he was unconscious. He was rushed to the nearest medical center for emergency treatment.

The staff found out that people were choking and fainting. One of the attendants carrying Husam asked, "What is going on here?"

The other attendant replied, "I have no idea."

They could see the staff attending to patients while a few were just recording the event using cell phones. The patients' eyes were rolling, they were undressed and water was thrown at them as they were agitated and restless. These two did not understand what was happening. However, they did what they were trained to do. Husam got a little glimpse of what was happening, but he thought that they were people who got injured by the shrapnel. He was in so much pain. He was partially conscious. He only took a peek at the hospital and what was going around. One of the doctors said, "We have no time to attend to lethal injuries, as we face a bigger threat—a chemical weapon attack."

"Sir, please attend to this patient. He is the only survivor," said the medical attendant.

The doctor eventually agreed and started the treatment. The two attendants still did not understand what was happening due to the chemical attack. They wanted to know more about the chemical attack.

The next thing Husam remembered was waking up in the Zaatari camp. He was transported amongst many other refugees. He lost his family members. Even if they were alive, they must have been transported to another refugee camp. He did not even know what had happened. His whole life was turned upside down in a moment. All he remembered was that some while ago, he was with his friends playing football. The next thing he remembered was that he lost one of his legs, and could never play football. This dreadful fact found a space in his heart as a scar. He developed post-traumatic stress disorder, as the events that happened a few months ago still made him restless and eventually resulted in a panic attack. The primary cause of his situation was that he could never play again. He used to inquire about his family members in the camp office, but he always returned sad and disheartened. He missed his younger sister, Fatima so much that tears came down whenever he felt alone.

The only thing he could do now was watch the other kids play together. While standing in a corner, he saw a truck with new refugees that was about to enter Zaatari. He saw a woman watching him closely, and then the security checkpoint stopped her. Husam just looked at her. She was in so much fear that even her body language was noticeable to Husam. He thought that maybe her pain was even deeper than his problems. He continues to watch the game and guided them. "Pass the ball. Don't hold it for much longer."

(2014, Damascus, Syria.)

A convoy of pickup trucks was stationed at Damascus, ready to pick up Syrians for transportation. A city once filled with a rich cultural heritage presently lay in ruins due to the civil war. Nearly half of the city's structure was wiped out by constant bombardment from mortar shelling. The Syrian citizens were forcefully sent to refugee camps as political warfare snatched their homes and families away. The United Nations deployed a pickup truck to transport the homeless people to safety in the nearby centers. The UN office representative was busy cross-checking the names on the checklist. After their verification, there were allowed to move. There were six refugees, including two women and four adults. They only carried a small bag, as it was the only thing that they could gather. The rest was probably destroyed or lost. The truck started its journey toward Mafraq, Jordan. On the way, all the passengers could see that what was once their home was now a ghost town, with only smoke and debris. No one knew how many bodies were lying under those demolished concrete structures. They knew nothing was left for them there, and they had to start a new journey in some place entirely new, though they had no idea where they were headed. As they crossed Damascus, the empty desert was visible with no life around.

The truck came to a halt near a Jordan border check post. The driver parked the truck near a corner, stepped out, carrying the document folder, and headed toward the check post for verification. He greeted the officer by saying, "*Salam.*"

The officer replied, "*Salam*" and handed over the documents to the officer. After going through the files and cross-checking them with the online server, he handed over the papers to the driver and said, "*Khuda hafiz.*"

The driver also greeted him back by saying "*Khuda hafiz.*"

The officer said, "I don't know how many more the camp can sustain."

The driver started walking toward the truck. The passenger did not know what was lying ahead in that desert. One of the Syrian men said, "They are taking us to Mafraq. They have a place over there for us."

Another man beside him replied, "It's called Zaatari!"

The rest of the group remained quiet. The truck started moving and reached the outskirts of Mafraq. The passengers finally saw a city with dwellings and people living their everyday life. The truck crossed the town and started moving toward the east of Mafraq. Within a few minutes, they reached their destination—the Zaatari refugee camp. Out of nowhere, the Syrians just saw a hugely-spread base in the vast empty desert. After seeing the center, one of the passengers said, "It is not a camp. It is a city."

The truck was parked near the camp's security post. The driver instructed them to move out of the car and handed over their Syrian documents for immigration and verification. The Zaatari refugee camp held the highest number of Syrian refugees outside Syria.

As the vehicle stopped before the camp office, teenage children were seen playing football. One of the Syrian women passengers saw a disabled boy standing in the nearby corner with the support of his crutches. He was constantly watching the football game that was being played nearby. From the way he was watching football, anyone could figure out how badly he wanted to play. Unfortunately, he could not. Women were sitting around the corner and were just watching everything and discussing. The woman who just arrived at the camp with the rest seemed very quiet, and her body language suggested that she was upset for some reason—as if she had lost something close to her heart, though she remained calm. She felt terrible for this young boy and wished she could help him with his struggle. The driver told them, "Ignore the look of the security guard. He always has his suspicion about everyone."

The camp security officer started verifying, and everyone was waiting in a queue. The woman's chance came finally.

The guard yelled, "Next!"

She moved forward with the documents in her small bag. The officer gave her a very unfamiliar look. He ordered, "Show me your ID."

She opened her little suitcase and took out her national ID. Only her eyes were visible as she was wearing a *hijab*. "Show me your face," the guard yelled again.

Feeling frightened, she uncovered her face. The guard matched her face with the ID card. "You are Nadia," he said.

She was a very fair-skinned woman, had a medium height, greenish eyes, and a squarish face. She looked like she was in her late 40s—not more than that. "Show me your family booklet," the guard said.

She was shivering as she handed over the pamphlet. "Where are they?" he asked.

She did not say anything. The guard just understood that nobody survived. "Move on," he said.

She grabbed the bag, put the documents inside, and moved toward her new home.

(Zaatari Refugee Camp, 2014)

Nadia was walking toward her new home. The camp was much organized in terms of living standards. There were permanent dwelling structures, a good market for all the daily needs and essentials, and even UNICEF had created schools for children to help them get free education. Nadia was happy to see such a well-maintained campaign for the Syrian people. She was allotted a house close to the market. She reached a place with external walls painted in olive green and had dish antennas installed on top of the walls. She never thought that she would be able to afford such luxuries again. She reached the main entrance of the house while carrying her limited belongings in her small bag which she had with her. She knocked on the door and waited. An old woman wearing a hijab greeted her by saying, "Welcome, my dear," and embraced her.

Nadia was not expecting such a warm welcome at all. She felt the warmth and affection of the elderly lady. Nadia greeted her back by saying, "Thank you so much."

"Come inside, my dear. It is boiling outside."

Nadia stepped in with some sign of relief. "My name is Rukhsana! Put your stuff there," she said and pointed at the corner beside her bed.

"Be at ease, my child. You must be exhausted from the journey. Make yourself comfortable, and oh, I forgot to ask your name."

"My name is Nadia."

Rukhsana said, "You are just like your name, beautiful. Well, this is your house now. We also work here in the market, and yeah, there is one more woman who stays with us—Nafisa. She could be here anytime."

Nadia just nodded her head in agreement. "Well, you relax and get settled. Hopefully, I will be joining you with Nafisa."

She smiled cheerfully and went out. Nadia thought Rukhsana was a caring and affectionate lady. She just sat near the chair, grabbed her bag, and started searching for something. Then she grabbed a cigarette, quickly lit it up, and started smoking while her eye was stuck on the door.

After a while, Rukhsana came inside the home along with Nafisa. Nadia was simply sitting in the corner. "Nadia, I want you to meet Nafisa."

Nafisa was about the same height as Nadia—about five feet tall, with a round face and light brown eyes. She was pleased to see someone her age. Nadia and Nafisa exchanged greetings with each other. "We work at the market. It's a perfect place. We will show you soon."

"I would love to go there, but what do you do there?" asked Nadia politely.

"We sell vegetables and other household stuff," said Rukhsana. "And Nafisa also assists me. She also has a boring part-timing job with some UN thing."

Nafisa laughed and said, "I'm a part-time volunteer for UNICEF."

"Oh! UNICEF, that's great," said Nadia.

"Let's all prepare supper," said the optimistic Rukhsana.

They all got engrossed in making a meal for dinner.

After settling down in her new home, she thought about how she could help people somehow. She came out of the house and sat near the door, observing the people. Again, she noticed the same boy whom she had seen at the security checkpoint the previous day. A young boy who was physically disabled was seen walking with his crutches. He had grown a beard, wore dirty clothes, and was carrying a few torn bundles of books in his bag. He sat in the same lonely spot daily and started reading a few books.

Local small boys could be seen playing football on the small field nearby. He was in distress, as he just watched boys playing football—which he could not play. The other local boys call him *Coach* which made him feel good. He wanted to play and be a part of a group of boys, but he tried to distance himself from others around him. When it came to football, he ditched everything. He tried to calm himself by reading books during the rest of his free time. He wanted to forget something which had happened to him. Husam has been at the camp for quite some time now. The young lad wanted to do something as he felt stuck in one place for too long. Nadia noticed the boy every day and felt terrible for him. She felt low, knowing his daily routine. Either he was guiding the young boys while they were playing or was reading in the same corner—sitting all alone. She thought that the Syrian refugees once had a home, family, and life. At present, they had nothing left. Still, life goes on, and the people were trying hard to adapt to that new adventure. But to her surprise, everyone was doing well. Nadia, too, was quite well settled in the new home. She was waiting for a few more days and then thought of telling Nafisa that she also wanted to work like her.

Nadia thought it was the right time to ask how they both ended up there. As dinner was over, it was the regular time for gossip and chit-chat. Nadia initiated the topic by carefully observing both of their behaviors. She asked, "I know I should not ask this, but how did you end up here?"

Nafisa's smile vanished and her face turned pale. She remained silent. Rukhsana replied, "I escaped from Darra after the shootout. My son

Moshin was the reason the protest started. Now he has become popular amongst the Syrian youth. He told me that I wasn't safe there and that he will come to pick me up one day. I'm waiting for him."

Nadia's expression now changed after listening to her about Mohsin. She remained silent. "I'm sorry, and I'm sure he will come for you," said Nadia reassuringly.

She turned toward Nafisa. She remained silent—as if she did not exist. Nadia asked her, "Are you all right, my dear?"

Rukhsana said, "Nafisa come on, if we have to stay under one roof together, we will not have any secrets. Tell her."

Nafisa started sobbing and said, "My worst nightmare is the camp itself. My husband died in Damascus just a few months after our marriage. Since I arrived here, I have been raped by many unknown people. I just want to leave this place somehow."

There was complete silence in the house. Nobody said anything. Nadia got up and hugged Nafisa. Rukhsana also joined. Due to the sad environment, they forget to ask about Nadia's past.

As they went to sleep, Nadia felt terrible for these women and everybody in that camp. She remembered an event from her past.

2011, London, United Kingdom, MI:5 Building (Undisclosed, Location.)

A young British lady was sitting at her desk and looking at a file on her laptop. She receives a message on her cell which said, *the asset is ready*. She quickly got up and rushed toward her chief's cabin. She was about to knock, but Mr. Richard Fieldon indicated that she should come inside. She said, "the asset is ready, Sir!"

Fieldon replied, "I hope he is. I don't want this to be messed up."

"It won't, Sir," she replied.

Fieldon interrupted her in between and said, "Rachel, this is way too big! Way above our pay grade. If something goes wrong, the whole agency will have to pay, including the both of us."

"I understand, Sir. We have done our groundwork," replied Rachel.

Fieldon nodded and Rachel went outside. He looked a little tense. She received another message—*How did it go?* She arrived at her desk, took a deep breath, and started typing—*It is a go*.

The CIA had been looking to infiltrate Syria for a long time. The Arab Spring movement gave the necessary elements of camouflage for the western mind to extract the resources of an oil-rich country by declaring that the leader was a dictator. The media coverage generally makes people believe that the leaders are inhuman and that citizens suffer. The news channel only shows a particular aspect that they are instructed to cover, which is not necessarily true. The CIA special sectary, Diana Francis contacted Richard Fieldon of MI5 for a secret mission. CIA was very clear about how they wanted to use the Arab Spring movement as a decoy to hatch a perfect conspiracy that would start a civil war in Syria. MI5 had clear instructions to plan a mission in which Syrian leaders would be portrayed as tyrants and would divide the people in a way that would benefit the Western ideology. Turkey was instructed to fund the rebellion group once the nation was in chaos. Saudi Arabia had to do the same by supporting rebel groups. Iran was the only ally left, and its intelligence was insufficient to stop the upcoming war.

Rachel was assigned the task of planning an invasion mission. She was a young, dynamic British analyst and was pretty good at her job. She was instructed to study the country's current affairs and devise a plan. Rachel started monitoring and looking at Syria from a different perspective. She propagated the idea that Syria would become like Iraq under Assad. She appointed new agents to provide vital information about the country. CIA also provided their assets which were deployed in Syria. MI5 and the CIA jointly worked on this mission. Rachel devised a very subtle plan. She targeted the youth for the initiation.

CIA already presented Rachel with Al-Rashid, a spiritual leader and a teacher in Darra. Rachel contacted Rashid through satellite phone and instructed, "I want a few young and rebellious boys who are well trained."

Rashid asked, "By well-trained you mean?"

"Can they paint?" asked Rachel.

"I'm sorry! Did I hear that right? Paint?"

"Yes, you heard that right. That's exactly what I want them to do."

"They know how to use a gun, make and plant the IED, but I don't think my boys know how to paint," said Rashid.

"Can they paint just a slogan?" asked Rachel.

After thinking for a couple of seconds, Rashid replied, "I thought my boys would perform something significant, but if you want them to paint, they will do that."

"Perfect then! Just train them well enough and I will provide them with the message that they need to paint! Where and when," said Rachel and hung up.

Rashid thought, ***what a waste of energy and resources!***

(Damascus, April 2011.)

A Syrian military leader was sitting in his chamber. He looked tense since he has just received intel that could destroy the entire nation. Nadir said, "Connect me to the President right now," on the intercom.

His secretary replied, "Right away, Sir."

While acknowledging the fact that the whole country would be adversely affected, Nadir said, "Our enemy has hatched a plot to overthrow you, Mr. President! They are already ahead of us. We will be hit at any moment."

Assad replied, "Do what is needed but protect our people."

Nadir replied, "I will do my best, Mr. President."

Nadir called for an emergency meeting, as he was the head of the intelligence of Syria. The staff gathered in the meeting hall. Nadir said, "Gentlemen, we are at war! What do you all have for me?"

One of the analysts said, "Sir, it's been confirmed that the British are working with the Saudis to infiltrate Syria."

"I know that. What else?" asked Nadir.

"They are trying to sabotage our President's image and portraying him as a dictator. They are here for the oil. CIA is involved, Sir," said the experienced Mazur, the most profound Director of Intelligence.

Mazur also stated, "If we don't act now, Sir, we will be cornered, as your allies are limited in number and your enemies are united."

Nadir acknowledged Mazur's interpretation of the whole situation. He said, "Deploy the army to counter those attacks. Get on it. Now! Damn it!"

(Daraa, Syria, 2011.)

Rashid called the young disciples and told them to prepare for a task. Mohsin was called upon. He was ready to die for the cause—Rashid's cause. Rashid told him, "Gather a few more boys and take some spray paint."

For a moment, Mohsin kept quiet and asked curiously, "Do we have to paint? That's it?"

"Mohsin, this is just the beginning. Understand that it is not a simple task. All of you will be detained, so be ready for it. Head toward your school and paint the message."

After his mentor's reassurance, he agreed and went for what he was told to do. Mohsin walked toward his old school with two other friends. He was carrying a small bag. They reached the school. The message was clear—they had to spray paint on a school wall. Mohsin and his friends took spray paints from their bags as he passed the school gate. Mohsin said, "It's time. It is time for a change! *Allah hu Akbar!*"

The others repeated the same lines, thus showing their clear determination and will to follow instructions from their mentor. They made the graffiti that said, *Ejak el door, ya doctor.* (Meaning: It's your turn, Doctor.) The message was meant for President Bashar al-Assad.

This young group of boys did not know that they would change the destiny of Syria and theirs too.

Meanwhile, Syrian secret service police known as the *Mukhabarat* gathered the intel that foreign forces had already penetrated Syria. These rebel forces were funded and supported by the CIA and the Saudis to help overthrow Assad. They knew the enemies had hired these young boys to split the Syrian rule. Nadir was sitting at his desk. Mazur knocked on the door and entered. He said, "My men have interpreted a message written on an old school wall—*Ejak el door, ya doctor!*"

Nadir replied, "They are referring to the President. Find out more! Arrest the ones who are responsible. Find out Mazur, what are they up to, now. We need to act fast. They are on to something huge."

Mazur replied, "On it, Sir, right away."

"And Mazur," Nadir called out.

He turned back. "Deploy the army. I smell danger. We should be ready for retaliation, and the response team should be ready," said Nadir.

"Yes, Sir," replied Mazur.

Mazur instructed his men by saying, "Go to Darra. Find out who's behind all this and send the army to Darra. We are at war. Get me the people who are responsible for this."

The team started getting ready for the mission. Mazur instructed the army personnel to be prepared. Mazur told them, "Do not engage until you are told. We don't know who the enemy is and where are they, but we know they are inside. So be prepared for anything."

"Sir," said the army officer, Jiyad and the *Mukhabarat* senior officer, Habibullah. The army battalion started its journey toward Darra. As Habibullah reached Darra, he told his men, "Find and arrest these youngsters. We need to know who is behind this and don't shoot at any cost—these are our people. Just get this vital intel without alerting the enemy. The task of the army is to avert any direct military attack."

Nadir's plan was simple—to know who was behind all that. However, the enemy's plan was very different. They had a plan to dethrone the President himself. CIA started the funding program under which the rebels were provided weapons and necessary combat training. MI5's task under Rachel's supervision was to infiltrate Syria and create a chaotic surrounding. She was informed that the army and the Syrian intelligence were moving toward Darra. She knew it was about time they would arrest those innocent boys for extracting any information. That was exactly what she wanted. It was part of her plan. She received another text message—*We are ready for Phase Two.* She replied by texting—*Good! Hold on!*

The special forces arrested Moshin who was accused of the graffiti act in a few days. Nadir made sure all the boys were interrogated lawfully. The army was stationed in Darra for any enemy attack. In the meantime, the global media house started reporting that Assad's regime was torturing the young boys just for wall graffiti. The news spread like fire in a wild forest. Within a month, the media ensured that Assad was a dictator and brought much global attention to Syria. Protests started in various parts of the country. Mohsin and the other boys were interrogated well enough, but the Intelligence only pulled out the hatred for the President. In the meantime, the Syrian rebel force called itself the **Free Syrian Army** captured the Syrian people's and government's attention. CIA did its job well. Nadir was summoned to the capital. "What is your plan to counter these upcoming protests? Or, rather threats?" asked President Assad calmly.

"The enemy has infiltrated the nation. Our intelligence has failed miserably and we cannot figure out these forces' actual plan," said the disappointed Nadir.

"Are you telling me that we are incompetent?"

"No! Mr. President. We have intercepted a few messages and we are working on a few leads," said Nadir, ensuring that he has been working day and night.

"Hmm! The protest in Darra should be conducted peacefully without any violence. Make sure of that." said the President reassuringly.

"Noted Sir," spoke Nadir.

Hundreds of protesters gathered in Darra's town. Nadir deployed the security personnel with just sticks and ensured that no weapon was used during the peaceful protest. The Syrians were carrying boards with a clear message of releasing a young teenager who was arrested for protesting. The voice was clear and shouted the slogan *release the innocent!* Nadir was observing every moment from a safe house nearby. Meanwhile, Rachel kept everything in London through trained assets, by recording every moment through spy cams. They were disguised as local people and were untraceable by Syrian intelligence. Rachel said, "It's time for Phase Two. It is a go."

Suddenly, gunshots were fired with a loud noise. Instantly, many people were torn apart by sniper bullets. "Snipers!" screamed Nadir.

"Run! Find them out now," he instructed his unit.

All of them ran to find the source of the snipers. The snipers were hiding in local buildings and rooftops. They remained undetectable. The shots were fired again. The protesters panicked and started running to get to safety. This panic resulted in a severe stampede. Many innocent lives were crushed under people's feet. The bodies were lying about and blood was streaming down the street. The Syrian army did not anticipate this sort of anarchy and confusion. There was a bloodbath. Nadir was utterly clueless. His men could not react faster. The sniper, who was very strategically placed, had initiated the attack and this event marked the birth of the civil war in Syria known as the *siege of Daraa*. Nations were divided the same way as had happened with Iraq. The Iranian intelligence agency had warned Syria of the upcoming threat, but they were not anticipating such an organized infiltration mission. This incident sparked the Syrian civil war.

Rachel and her team were seated in London and they crafted a script that would decide the future of millions of Syrians. She watched the whole scene just happening in front of the projector screen with the other members of the agency. Somehow, she did not feel right about it. Her mother's ideology took over her logical mind. The agency and Richard Fieldon congratulated her for her analytical skills and how she executed the whole plan. Rachel Green, born to an Englishmen, George Green, and a British-Libyan mother, Farah Sheikh, considered herself more British than Libyan. Since her childhood, she had been brilliant. After completing graduate school, she was spotted by an agency talent spotter, who recommended her profile. Soon after graduation, she became a top analyst at MI5. Her father was a reputed lawyer and a council in the British government, while her mother was a gynecologist at St. George's hospital.

Rachel did not like what she did today, though she was trained for such missions. How those snipers penetrated and tore apart Syrians today impacted her heart, but her mind told her a different story. She was also proud of her father. She was so well and had spotlessly conducted everything that even the CIA praised her. She returned home and was greeted by her mother, who had just come down. Mr. Green was busy watching the news on his couch in the living room.

The news described how President Assad and his army killed hundreds of his people to show his power. The news agency declared Assad was a dictator and comparisons were drawn with Saddam Hussain immediately. He said, "Yet another Gulf scum."

Farah disapprovingly said," Those are people who just died there! Just like you and me."

"He killed his people's people. Can't you see that?" said George.

"You don't know that yet," said Farah.

Rachel stared at her mother with suspicion as though her secrets had been spilled outside. Farah continued, "These Americans must need oil again. For the sake of oil, I don't know how many innocent lives will be crushed to death. They did it in the past and will do it again."

"You are British National first. Never forget that. We have been grateful to this great nation regarding border policy. We accepted everyone coming from every continent," said George with an affirming voice.

"It is not about Britain or Libya. It's about humanity. What is happening to Muslims living around the globe is not justifiable," said Farah getting highly emotional over her husband's remark.

Rachel tried to calm things down by intervening and saying, "Guys, it is not our war. We don't know anything about Syria. Mom, please don't worry. Everything will be all right."

She pointed toward her father so as not to make any more remarks.

The whole family set aside their differences for supper. That night, Rachel felt her mother was right somewhere. The sight of a sniper shooting Syria was disturbing her and not letting her sleep. She entered her mother's room. Farah worked on some medical files that were on her laptop. She asked, "Everything all right, sweetie?" Rachel replied," I can't sleep, Mom."

Farah embraced her. Rachel lay in her lap to get some solace.

Chapter 12

Revelations

(Zaatari Refugee Camp, 2014.)

As Nadia was getting familiar with her new environment, she felt the need to do something to earn a living and not just waste her time in activities such as sitting and chatting. She had already instructed Nafisa to fix a meeting with UNICEF. After a few weeks, Nafisa came home from work one day and she did not find Nadia, searched for her and called her name, "Nadia, Nadia! Where are you hiding? You dumb woman!"

They both had developed a bond of friendship. She finally knew where she must be. She went upstairs where they used to dry clothes and found Nadia smoking again. "Nadia! I knew you would be here."

She was happy to see her new friend. Nadia said, "Did you miss me?"

She passed the cigarette. Nafisa laughed, hesitatingly refused, and said, "Once you are done smoking, come down. I have some news for you."

"Tell me here before the old lady comes home."

They giggled, and Nafisa said, "You have to be at the UNICEF office by tomorrow noon sharp."

Nadia was happy, and she thanked her by hugging her tightly and passing the cigarette to her. Nafisa said, "no."

They both laughed and went downstairs.

The following day Nadia woke up early. There was a sense of excitement in her body language, which was visible. Nafisa and Rukhsana were also pleased to notice her in such a way. Nafisa said, "See you at the office by noon and please don't be late for the meeting."

They both left for the market. After a while, she thought of wrapping up her smoking before leaving. She was smoking upstairs and saw the same boy sitting in the corner reading something. She finally thought that it was time she talked to him. She got ready, looked at the mirror, and told herself, *you can do this.* She stepped out of the house and took a deep breath. She walked toward the boy and saw him getting a little concerned as he was not used to talking to strangers apart from his young football disciples. Husam hesitated to see her presence next to him. Although he had seen her many times before, he remembered seeing her entering the camp for the first time. Nadia asked politely with a smiling face, "What is your name?"

He replied, "Husam," after a pause.

"That is such a great name. So, what are you reading, Husam?"

After feeling a little at ease, he said, "It's just world history."

"So, you enjoy reading, hmm," said Nadia.

"No, I don't!" responded Husam quickly. "I'm out of options."

Nadia soon realized that he was talking about his leg. Nadia promptly tried to make him comfortable by saying, "Reading and getting to know about history is quite a cool job."

Husam replied, "Maybe."

"Hey, would you like to join some class to know more about the history and other cool stuff on—whatever you like," she asked.

Husam never thought anybody would ask him what he wanted to do at present. He felt a little involved and said, "Who would teach me?"

"I would, and there are many more to make you learn cool things."

Husam smiled a little but did not say anything. "Is that a yes, Mr. Coach?"

Husam was pleased with how she addressed him and said, "How did you know my actual name?"

She laughed and said, "I know a few things about you."

Husam felt better, and he eventually agreed to join her soon. "See you soon at the class," said Nadia and she left for her interview.

While on her way to the UNICEF desk, she noticed how the people had adapted to their new life. It was way better organized than a small rural town. Many international organizations ran the camps, such as UNICEF, to look after education. The World Food Program looked after the regular food supply, and health was looked after by Jordan Health Aid Society International in collaboration with UNHCR. Everything was available, but still, there was nothing. She reported sharp at noon in the UN office. She was waiting at the main reception and she looked around for Nafisa as she had organized the meeting with her superior. She waited for a few minutes. She was just looking around when she saw a giant logo of the United Nations on the wall. She could see pictures of visitors who visited the camp. They were not ordinary visitors, so they were mentioned in the Hall of Fame. She could recognize a few of them. "Nadia, you are here. Wonderful! Just wait for a while. I will have my supervisor here soon," said Nafisa after seeing Nadia scanning the Wall of Fame.

Nadia just smiled at her friend and waited for further instructions. Nafisa finally called her down. "Just follow me, and I hope you didn't smoke while coming," she said and they both smiled at each other.

"Now listen, Asma is a very sensible woman. Don't try to act smart in front of her. Just be honest and the work will be done."

"Yes, I will try," said Nadia and she smiled as she walked toward the door of Asia.

"She is waiting for you. Just go inside."

She saw a woman wearing a hijab, sitting at her desk, and reading some files as she entered the room. "*Salam*," said Nadia.

"Nadia, right?" the woman asked.

Nadia simply nodded her head. "Have a seat, dear."

Nadia sat and waited for a further round of questions. "So you were in the capital?"

Nadia replied, "Yes."

"Oh, you were a teacher in the capital, wonderful. I can offer you more than a volunteer's job."

Nadia was hopeful about a teacher's job but did not say anything. "Would like to teach some of the children in the camp?"

Nadia could not control her joy. She smiled and said, "I would love to teach again if given an opportunity."

Asma interrupted her by saying, "But there is a slight problem, Nadia. I can't assure you'll get the job until you fulfill one condition. If you can fulfill a condition then the job can be yours."

Nadia's joyful expression on her face faded away a little. Still, she remained calm and asked, "What guarantees do you need?"

"There is only one problem. The job is assured if you can get enough students to attend your class, and then you have my approval."

Nadia felt relieved and said, "I will try to fulfill this task."

"Great! I offered the job to Nafisa, but she wasn't as interested in it as you. I think you are the ideal candidate. Try gathering your students and the job is yours."

Nadia "Yes, Asma, I will do my best, and thank you so much."

Asma smiled back and thought she had found the perfect person.

Nadia felt so relieved to know that she had a new opportunity at hand, but it was not yet complete as she had to make many efforts to gather a whole bunch of students. She immediately thought of **Coach** Husam. Despite being disabled, the youth had a good fan base among his young disciples—the footballers. She returned home with a sad face and pretended to be disappointed. She knocked at the door, and Rukhsana opened it joyfully. "Did you get the job, my dear?" she asked.

As soon as she saw her face, she thought she was rejected and said, "Don't worry, there will be other openings my dear. You can give me a hand in my business."

A voice was just heard saying, "She is messing with you, Rukhsana. She has got the job. She only needs to find a few students," said Nafisa observing everything from above.

Nadia smiled and said, "You are such a spoilsport. You don't have any sense of humor."

Rusksana said, "You both are the same."

They all smiled and returned to their work.

The following day Nadia knew where to find Husam. She went to check whether Husam was there or not, and indeed he was there—right opposite her house, gazing at books in the usual manner. She quickly went toward him to offer him a deal where both would gain something. Husam saw her coming, smiled, and before she could request him to gather a few students, he said, "How was your interview, Sister?"

She felt touched by his statement, and to hear him call her *sister*, filled her heart with overwhelming joy. She was also surprised at how he came to know about it. She said surprisingly, "How did you know that?"

"I have my spies in every corner in this camp," said Husam.

"Then you also must know about the outcome of my interview," said Nadia.

She started to enjoy this conversation. "Sit, Sister, please sit," said Husam.

"You know you are not the only person who was offered this job. There were many before you. They failed to gather the naughty footballers so they could sit and study," said Husam.

Nadia thought the young boy was not dumb. He was pretty intelligent and observant of his surroundings. Nadia sat next to him as one of his disciples and said, "Will you help me, my Lord, in lending your followers to follow me in the holy route of learning?"

Husam laughed loudly and said, "Yes, my Lady, they will follow and so will I."

They both laughed.

Finally, Nadia had the guts to ask him about his leg. "What happened to your leg?" asked Nadia softly.

Husam's laughter diminished suddenly, but somehow, he thought of telling her about the incident which took away his life.

He said, "I'm sure you must have heard of Ghouta. Did you know what happened there?"

The word Ghouta made her so uncomfortable that her face became red and she started sweating. Husam was about to share the details with her, but suddenly a voice interrupted their intense conversation. "Coach, you are needed in the field right now," said one of the young boys who came there to call his coach, Husam.

"Yes, I'm coming," said Husam.

He gathered his crutches, got up, and addressed Nadia by saying, "Don't worry Sister, you will get the job."

Nadia was still in some distress, but somehow, she managed to say, "Thank you, brother."

Husam smiled and started moving toward the field with the young lad. Meanwhile, Nadia was still lost in some troubling thoughts from her past.

Nadia was not over her past events, but she knew that she had to get to her new life for her betterment and the people she had directly affected. Now, her only priority was to get a job somehow. For a change, in the next few days, Husam was not spotted in the same place as he used to be. Not seeing him there made Nadia feel a little worried. She wondered, *where did he go?* Nafisa was holding a letter in her hand while Nadia was busy smoking upstairs. "I think they must have rejected you," said Nafisa in a cheerful manner.

Nadia smiled and said, "Hmm, probably."

Nafisa handed over the letter and said, "Open it."

Nadia opened the envelope and started reading the letter. To Nadia's surprise, the letter clearly stated that the job was offered to Nadia and that confirmation was awaited from her side. She thought about how the condition had been fulfilled. *How did she have the required students for attendance?* These questions popped into her mind, though she was happy knowing about the job. Nafisa already knew that Nadia had made it through. "You have got the job, you dumb woman, come. Come on, cheer up and get ready fast. We have to go work together," she said.

Nafisa tried to control her excitement. They both laughed and looked at each other. Rukhsana observed both her roommates carefully and was thrilled with joy. She treated them as though they were her family members. She said, "Will you not hug your old member in your secret mission?"

They both rushed downstairs and hugged Rukhsana. Tears of bliss started flowing down her eyes—as if her old, lost family had been reunited with her. Rukhsana said, "Let us all go to work together."

"Yes, we should! Let us go, guys. I don't want to be late on my first day at work," replied Nadia.

They all start moving toward the market.

As they reached the market, Rukhsana reached her shop, and Nafisa stayed with her as she would assist her during the first half of the day. Nadia walked toward the UNICEF camp. She was handed over some new ID cards and files when she reached the primary office. She got to her classroom and found it to be full of youngsters who were shouting and giggling with each other. Husam was sitting in one corner on a stool.

Nadia was indeed pleased to see so many students who were gathered together. She pointed toward Husam to make everybody quiet and listen to her. Husam instructed the group of boys and girls to be silent. Nadia said, "Thank you all for joining the class. I'm Nadia and I will be your new teacher. Let us begin the first day in class. We will be learning about world history today. So, are you ready?"

All of them yelled "Yes!"

They were interested and excited to start something new. The children's parents were also happy when they heard that some educational classes were about to begin, as these children would waste their precious time roaming here and there, but now things were getting sorted out. In the afternoon, they would study and learn a few things. In the evening, they would play football.

After a few days, Nadia thought of thanking Husam for his efforts in bringing those children together. Husam used to sit in the same place, but presently, he was interested in knowing world history. He was sitting and reading something. Nadia said, "Thank you, Husam. Because of you, I got this job."

"Don't thank me just yet. It's just the beginning. You will have to conduct more than one class," said Husam.

Nadia felt glad that she saw hope and optimism in Husam. He said, "That day, you asked me what happened to my leg. Well…it is a long story."

Nadia thought she could not avoid that conversation forever, so it was better to let him finish. Husam continued his story "I used to live in Ghouta with my family. My father was a carpenter and my sister just graduated from college. My mother used to take care of all of us. We were a happy family and it was all going well until the fight began. We had been isolated from Damascus, the capital city. The rebel force made Ghouta their base camp to fight against the government. We never had any issues with our president, but then we heard how the young boys were assaulted just for some stupid graffiti. My family didn't pick any side. All we ever wanted was to get shifted to Damascus somehow and live a normal life. Then, on one fine day, we played football like any other day, but they attacked us with missiles and mortar. We ran toward our home, feeling scared, and suddenly a shell exploded in the nearby car. The next thing I remember was waking up in a hospital with my leg gone. I must tell you the worst part of it, or rather the most interesting part of it. I was not fully conscious, but I did see these medical staff in a hurry to gather as many injured people as possible, and I swear I had seen them exposing the chlorine gas to the people who started hallucinating and were unconscious. Many of the medical staff were busy recording the incident. They were throwing water on the patients who were exposed to the gas to make it more real. The poor people did not realize that they were just being used for cinematic purposes. The next thing I remember was getting a pair of crutches and being sent to this mess. Later, I read the news about *Sarin*, the chemical nerve agent that Assad used against us. I laughed at how these amateur actors carried out a play and fooled the entire world into believing that some chemical weapons had attacked us. There was no gas attack, only chlorine. Can you imagine that? The most ironic part was that the entire world believed it was real. Syria was never so advanced that it would develop chemical weapons. We just saw a cell phone a few years ago, when it was a simple device for the rest of the world. Believe me, Sister, they fooled us, and we were not even laughing."

Nadia started sweating and said, "It's too hot today…isn't it? That is a hard fact to digest. I mean, who could do such a thing? Even I personally thought it was a terrifying incident. We heard stories that the chemical attack was real, and Assad did it. This is shocking and disturbing at the same time. I thought it was all real—whatever the media showed us."

"No, absolutely not. They have been lying from the beginning. They are here for oil and gas—what else? They did the same thing with Iraq and many other Gulf countries. Unfortunately, it was our turn."

Nadia felt that Husam was way too exposed to everything at a very young age. She said, "I'm sorry about your leg, Husam. I wish I could have helped you, but you should never lose hope. Trust me, everything will be all right one day."

Husam said, "I hope so. It is my football-guiding time."

Nadia was waiting for that conversation to get over. As soon as Husam was gone, Nadia just sat there remembering something about the Ghouta incident.

(London United Kingdom 2012)

After the Darra Incursion was successful, Rachel did get her fair share of appreciation back in London. However, the whole plan did not go as per the script. Syria resisted the attack, and it managed to overcome the invasion plan to a certain extent. Syria was well backed by Russia and Iran, putting the CIA's program on hold as they had to develop something slightly more innovative and probably dramatic. Rachel was directly summoned by the CIA operations chief, Diana in London. Diana said, "Good job in successfully converting the Darra peace protest into an invasion. Our Intelligence team suggests that it wasn't enough. Our enemies now have the edge over us. I want you to come up with something bigger this time than Darra so that Assad is cornered. Our resources are at your disposal."

Rachel was just listening calmly. She was a little upset with the incident, but it was her job to analyze the data and follow orders. "I will do my best, Ma'am, but Darra turned out to be too violent. Many innocent lives were lost. This time around, I will try minimal collateral damage," said Rachel.

"That is not your job, Rachel, and neither is it mine. Your job is to come up with something that will help us overthrow Assad. That is all. Syrians are not our concern. Do you understand? Just say no if you can't fulfill the task because we can't afford failure," said Diana commandingly.

Rachel realized that they would get it done either way, whatever they wanted, so saying 'no' was not an option. She asked, "I will give you what you want and not let people die this time. Sorry Ma'am, I did not mean that, but I need to be in Syria with my team on the ground, and I will need intensive media to support me this time at my command."

Diana replied, "Now you are talking like a Mi5 agent. Don't let your emotion overpower your intellect. I have seen many people falling for this act and paying unimaginably. You will have whatever you require for this mission."

"I'm already on it," said Rachel as she started moving toward her desk.

That night, Rachel told her parents that she was heading toward Dubai for some urgent work and that she would be back within a few months. Her mother, Farah, was worried and insisted that she should not go. She felt that something was not right with how she was leaving for Dubai all of a sudden. Mr. Green thought there was something important. They did not know that she worked at Mi5. For them, she was working for the ministry of external affairs. It was against the protocol even for the immediate family to know anything about the secret service. Rachel left for Damascus with no plans on how would she be able to fulfill the promise that she made to Diana. Rachel was given new IDs and documents. As per her new identity, she was Emily Fletcher, a media reporter who worked for CNN news. She was assigned a new team who were a mix of both agencies. She was stationed at Damascus. After seeing the condition of the city, she was heartbroken. The city was in ruins. The people had to choose a side, not by choice—it was forced upon them by more powerful and lustful nations, which craved more power. Her team was assigned a workstation in an old apartment building which was half destroyed by constant bombardment. Her instruction was clear—she had to devise a plan that would occupy center stage, and the world's reaction would create a diversion that the CIA would take advantage of immediately. As she started interacting with the locals to gather intelligence as a TV reporter, she held herself responsible for their fate more than anyone else. The fire crushed so many innocent lives, but the western nations' greed was immense, and she was here to put more fuel to the fire. She remembered not to let her emotion take control of their intelligence, but it was too late, as she already held herself responsible. Slowly, her intellectual mind was getting overpowered by a strong surge of emotions which was not good for her mission. She made up her mind that no lives would be taken this time around. There was enough intelligence gathered for her to come up with another plan. This time, she scripted an attack that could overthrow Assad within months. The data suggested that the percentage of Syrians hating its president was less than the immense love people had for him. That was it—that percentage was to be changed. To make Assad look like a dictator in the world on a global platform, he had to be made to do things that dictators do, generally. Rachel devised a tactical mission plan in which a new Syrian army, the newly formed rebel group stationed in Ghouta, would be attacked by Assad's forces. Assad's forces frequently attacked the rebel forces, which was not new, so Rachel added some flare—*Sarin,* in the shadow of this attack. When exposed to the atmosphere, a nerve agent leads to choking, fainting, and death of the recipient as an extreme result. Rachel and her team reached Ghouta. She gave instructions to her team on what was to be done. She knew when Assad's forces would start the shelling as per the intel. It did happen as planned—bombs started hitting the city. Rachel and her team were waiting for the injured to arrive at the medical facility and the action would begin. All the medical staff members were given money and instruction on what to do. The injured people started arriving in ambulances, but this time around, the treatment had an element of drama. All of them were given a healthy dose of chlorine gas, which resulted in rolling eyes and choking. Many victims started fainting. Little children were also exposed to the gas, which had a terrible effect on them. Patients were given oxygen, and water was thrown at them—it all looked so real. However, Rachel's team was busy recording the event, which looked like people were exposed to a chemical gas. None of the medical staff was wearing masks. If anyone was exposed to some form of nerve gas, it could have an equal impact on everyone. These videos were quickly distributed to all the international news agencies. The world believed that Assad attacked its people with a *Sarin* nerve agent. In reality, there was no *Sarin* in the first place— only fabricated lies. Rachel's mission was a success, but her heart felt disgusted with her act. The situation made her doubt herself and her mind raised a few questions. *How many lives have to be lost in the name of freedom? And freedom from what?* They were not liberated but forcibly plunged into misery in the name of freedom. She broke down, after looking at the innocent children who were receiving treatment. These people were merely used as objects. They were not even given a chance to escape. She was overwhelmed with emotions. She somehow decided to help the people. She destroyed all her old documents by burning them. She gathered her team and told them that there was another important assignment for which she would have to get a new identity. There was a man whom she trusted. She told Martin she was done with destruction. Martin knew her well and her current state of mind. Rachel said, "Martin, please, please forge some new IDs. Make sure it is of Syria this time."

Martin was shocked and said, "Rachel have you lost your mind? Are you going to stay here? Really?"

Rachel said, "I have seen enough. I can't lie back and watch that I'm the person who is destroying the very basis of the existence of these people. I have committed the worst crime. I know God will never forgive me for my action. But I will not follow this path anymore. Can you do it for me or not, Martin?"

Martin knew it would not end well for her. He said, "You know the drill and what exactly happens to a rogue agent."

"I know what will happen to me. Don't worry about me, no matter the cost, but I have to do it. So, are you helping me or not?" said Rachel.

"I will do it, Rachel, and I can protect you to an extent, but they will find you and come for you, no matter where you hide."

"I know," replied Rachel.

Martin created fake IDs for Rachel, and she became Nadia—a Syrian citizen. Rachel went missing after the Ghouta incident. Martin updated the agency many days later, deliberately delaying and slowing down the whole process as Rachel went missing and was currently out of sight.

Chapter 13

Dead End

Back in London, Diana and Fieldon were praising Rachel Green, the woman who divided Syria. President Obama suggested a strong attack would be taken against Assad for the chemical attack on its people. The people's opinion became anti-Assad propaganda, and the media declared him to be a dictator. Now comparisons were drawn with Saddam Hussein. Syria would probably face the same fate as Iraq. The United Nations launched an inquiry into the incident and claimed that more than a thousand people were dead. Yes, people were dying but not of anything related to chemical warfare. The ugly truth was kept hidden from the mainstream world. Diana and the whole agency were busy developing new plots for the war, and it was confirmed that Rachael had been missing for weeks. Diana doubted that her emotions might have overpowered her rational thinking. She only hoped that she did not do anything stupid. Soon, the agency would start hunting for her.

Nadia realized that Husam was in the same hospital when she was busy recording the incident and glorifying it as a chemical attack. She felt guilty about Husam's condition and thought she had to somehow help him out of that mess. He could never have guessed she was present in the same building where he was getting treated, though he did see many details of what was happening. Who would listen to and believe that disabled boy? Nadia only had one thing on her mind. She had to help as many of those people as possible. Her classes did not go unnoticed. She became popular among the young learners. Asma was praised for identifying Nadia as the perfect teacher. This news spread across the whole camp, and the security guard, who looked at everyone with a suspicious eye said, "Let me visit her, this so-called teacher."

One day as the class got over, the guard was waiting for an opportunity to learn more about Nadia. When he saw her in the office, he recognized her immediately. *Was she the same woman who came many months ago?* He remembered her face. He started following her and eventually stopped her while walking toward her home. He asked her, "So you are the one people talked about? You are becoming quite popular for a newcomer."

Nadia hesitantly asked, "Is there a problem?"

He started staring at her uncomfortably.

Nadia's instinct told her what would happen next. She decided that she would teach him a lesson that day. Probably he was one of the men who raped the poor, helpless Nafisa. Seeking an opportunity, he tried forcing himself upon her and dragged her to an ally. He did not have any idea who was he messing with at that moment.

As no one was in the vicinity, Nadia punched him so hard that the guard fell. The force with which the strike came, was something that he did not anticipate. She hit and kicked him again and again. She was well trained in hand-to-hand combat. She did not stop there. She was about to break his leg, as the poor guy was severely injured. He never thought he would be thrashed in such a manner. He understood it the hard way. Nadia said, "Get up and get out of here. Don't show me your face again. If I see you around any woman, I will break both your balls. You won't even stand up if I see you around again."

He got up somehow, gathering the remaining strength that he had, and ran away. He thought, *how can a teacher beat the hell out of him? Is she even a teacher?* She was well trained for a combat situation. These stupid people must have given him the wrong information, but he thought he would seek revenge when the time was right. Nadia also realized that she should not have beaten him so badly—not that she regretted beating him. Her only concern was that the guard knew she was not a regular woman. He would be more suspicious and alert of her now, which could reveal her true identity.

As the days passed, Nadia worked hard for her students in the camp. Meanwhile, back in London, Mi5 had declared Rachel Green a threat to the agency, as she carried so much vital information that might compromise the whole agency. Diana and Fieldon were discussing how to trace her and get her back. As per the source, she was last detected at Ghouta hospital. Diana said, "Someone has helped her in running away. The question is why is she gone as a rogue? Is she a double agent?"

Fieldon replied, "She was the best agent we had. I'm still unable to digest the fact that she has gone missing. Maybe she has been killed in action or something like that. She would never run away like that."

"Whatever the reason might be, we still have to trace her. She knows way too much," said Diana.

"Let us send a search team to Syria," said Fieldon.

"Hmm, yes, we should," replied Diana.

Fieldon assigned two of his agents the task of going to Damascus and finding her somehow before it was too late. Jacob and Amanda were sent to the Syrian Capital in search of Rachel Green. They, too, were disguised as TV media reporters. Their only task was to trace her somehow. After landing in Damascus, they met Martin, who took over Rachel's rank. Martin gave them the file and told them to stay low. No one could be trusted in that country. People were raising the threat level. Martin knew those two could locate her, so he intentionally passed the information to the rebels and mercenaries' group, only to save her and delay the search mission, but he did not anticipate the repercussion that his decision would have on him.

Tariq, the leader of ISIS, received the information that two agents had come to Syria and acted as media personnel. He hatched a plan for his organization and was ready to give an interview to the international media. Martin told Jacob and Amanda that it was an excellent opportunity to find intel on Rachel and ISIS. They were both fooled into a trap. After a brief discussion, they agreed to take an interview with the leader, Tariq bin Nihad. They started their preparation, and

Tariq was waiting for them to show up. The journalists were picked up from a spot on the outskirts of Damascus. The van picked up Jacob and Amanda, and their eyes were covered as they could not remember the hideout location. Little did they know that they were getting abducted. They reached the safe house in an undisclosed location, where Tariq was waiting for them. The driver got out of the van and instructed them to step out of the truck. They were escorted into the premises. Their hands were tied behind their backs as they entered a dark room, where Tariq was sitting on a chair. He instructed his henchmen to uncover their eyes. They both got terrified by the sheer ambiance of the room, which was filled with terror and tension. They felt more scared just by looking at Tariq, who was wearing black clothes. He had a long beard, and if looks could bring fear to our hearts, then it was him. He held an Ak-47 rifle. They forget their task and what they were there for at that time. Tariq asked, "Do you know why you are here?"

Jacob was scared but replied, "We are here for the interview, just like you asked for."

"Interesting, but what do you know now about journalism?" asked Tariq.

They were even more terrified and remained quiet. "Tell me something. Why are you here? Then we might go easy on you," said Tariq.

Jacob's speech started, and he said, "We are just here to ask you a few questions, that is it."

Tariq smiled sickly, saying, "You do want to play games. Okay, as you wish."

He instructed his henchmen to beat them. They were locked up in an isolated chamber and tortured for many days. They were treated harshly, and Tariq knew they would break down very soon. After almost a week, Jacob said that he was ready to talk. He was brought to the same room where he met Tariq for the first time. Tariq spoke, "I asked you politely, but you didn't listen. Now tell me, why are you here?"

Jacob's face was unrecognizable. He was beaten pretty severely. He spoke out of fear and said, "We are searching for a woman—a British woman from the secret service. We fear that she might be a rouge or a double agent."

"Oh, your great nation is also involved. So, tell me more about this agent."

Jacob told him how Mi5 and the CIA had planned a joint mission to overthrow President Assad and take over the control of Syria. He also narrated how Rachel did all that initially. Tariq was so enraged that he almost choked Jacob with his bare hands. He said, "Give me all that you know about her and you might live."

Jacob handed over all the intel he had of Rachel, which included her intel—from photographs to videos. Tariq asked, "Where the hell are you?" while looking at Rachel's picture.

Tariq ordered a search in every part of Syria to find Rachel. ISIS was on it as it was time for them to teach her a lesson. ISIS's covert mercenariness was deployed into every corner of Syria, searching for Rachel Green.

Zaatari Refugee Camp 2015

As a teacher, Nadia taught her students typical school subjects. She was assigned Geography and History classes, which the students enjoyed the most. She had a knack for teaching, and students waited for her class to begin. Apart from teaching them normal subjects, she was an excellent counselor, unlike the other teachers. She regularly discussed students' problems, tried turning them into possibilities, and guided them. She tried turning them into options and taught them the solutions to their problems regularly. Soon, she became very popular amongst the students.

Nadia felt her educational classes would help those children, but she needed something more significant than what she was doing right then. She wondered about whom she could contact. She immediately thought of calling Martin. Looking for an opportunity, she sneaked to the rooftop and connected with Martin via a satellite phone, which was undetectable for a specific number of minutes. Martin was already in despair due to Jacob and Amanda's leak, which he made to protect Nadia. The mission failed miserably, and Martin held himself responsible. He received a call on his cell phone. It was none other than Rachel. "Where the hell are you?" asked Martin.

"It doesn't matter…Listen…," replied Rachel.

"No…You listen to me. Damn it! I lied to the agency to protect you, and now I'm screwed because of you, Jacob and Amanda…," said Martin, interrupting her in between.

"Tell me, what has happened to them?" asked Rachel.

"I made them go through a perilous path. They were here to find you. I shared this information with my sources, and ISIS somehow got a hold of it. They managed to manipulate us into believing that they were ready to cooperate with us. They agreed to make arrangements for an interview. Jacob and Amanda went for the interview to find out if you were a double agent or something. Instead, they were captured and tortured for weeks, and I think your life is in danger. ISIS is coming for you. They now know what you did in the past and will not spare you."

Rachel said, "Calm down, Martin. Don't worry about me. I know my fate very well. I need something from you. One last favor, Martin. That's it."

"Tell me what you need," replied Martin.

"Connect me with Diana as soon as possible. You know I don't have much time. Can you do that for me?"

"Yes, I can. Give me some time. Call me tomorrow. I will get in touch with you and connect you with her."

"Thanks, Martin."

She hung up the phone. Nadia did some digging at night. She did not sleep. She came across a US policy in which Syrians were allowed to enter the border of American soil. She knew it—this was it. She decided that night that she would ask Diana to put Husam and Nafisa's names on the list. At least they would have an opportunity to have a better life and future.

The ISIS informant reached the Zaatari refugee camp. He came along with a few other members. Everyone in the center was scared of hearing the mere name of the Islamic state. He approached the main gate of the camp. Everyone around started fleeing, seeing the flag on the truck waving before them. People felt it was indeed a bad situation, seeing them. The guard began begging for mercy. The mercenary said, "Have you seen this woman?"

The guard barely has the guts to look upwards. He managed to somehow look at the picture. His eyes were amazed to look at the picture. It was Rachel's picture, and the guard could not forget the face that beat him. He got up and said, "Yes, I have. She is right here. She is a teacher in the school. I doubt that she is a mere teacher."

The mercenaries were alerted after receiving the information. He asked, "Are you sure she is the woman? If you are playing a game, it will be your last."

"Why would I lie? I don't want to die. Once, I tried to be her forcefully. She knows how to fight. I can guarantee that she is the one," replied the guard.

The mercenary contacted Tariq and told him that someone had identified her. Tariq told him to be very careful. She could be armed and dangerous. He said, "Step into the camp in normal clothes. Keep an eye on her. I'm sending in the reinforcement. Make sure you don't lose her. If you do, I will kill you with my bare hands, clear?"

"Yes, Sir, I'm on it."

He instructed the guard and his team according to what the leader had commanded. They started moving toward the school, disguised as ordinary citizens. They saw her teaching in the school, and she was the same woman whose pictures he had seen many times. It was her. He informed Tariq that she was the one and they were spying on her. Tariq told them, "Don't do anything stupid. She is a trained agent."

That night, Nadia contacted Martin at the time he asked for her to get in touch. Martin connected Rachel and Diana. Diana asked, "Where the hell are you, Rachel?"

"I'm in the Zaatari refugee camp, Diana. I know I don't have much time. I just want to help these people. I have literally played with their lives. I don't have the right to do that. It is because of me that they are homeless and begging for life."

Diana knew what Rachel must have been through and how circumstances must have changed her perception. She said, "You know I can't help you. You have disobeyed and left the agency. I know you are no threat, but…"

"I don't need your help, Diana…these people do. I just want you to add a few names to the list of refugees who may be allowed to enter the US," said Rachel.

"Are you out of your damn mind? Do you think the US will allow anyone to enter their land?" asked Diana.

She was not happy with the sort of help that Rachel asked for at that time. Rachel said, "They are not just anyone—they are just people. There is one disabled young boy and two women. How are they a threat to your nation? Damn you! I gave up everything for your mission, and you just can't do anything. You just sit back and enjoy these people's death, ruthless scum…"

Diana thought for a few seconds and said, "Just three, give the names to Martin. Be careful, Rachel. I have intel that they know where you are now. I'm sorry you had to go through this, but I can't help you. That's what we do, Rachel. Emotions are the problem, but I'm not mad at you. It is just that you chose the wrong route. Goodbye, Rachel, and I wish I could have helped you more."

Rachel handed over the names to Martin. She cried a lot that night but was happy for Husam, Nafisa, and Rukhsana as they would have a better life than others in the camp.

Diana had the names now. She instructed her team to do the needful. She felt awful for Rachel as she was close to meeting her fate. The mercenaries gathered. They were waiting for the backup force to arrive. Nadia was conducting regular classes in her school. The ISIS mercenaries started moving toward the school. Screams were heard as the terrified Syrians started running in fear after seeing the Islamic state's fighters who were carrying guns and swords. This act was a message to put fear into the hearts of the Syrians and the world.

Nadia sensed that something was coming. She instructed her students to lay low and get to cover. They panicked. Nadia knew that they had arrived. She knew that it was time to face them. She looked at Husam and told him, "Don't worry, Brother. God has a much better plan for you. One day, you will be in a much better place than this, and you will be doing what you always loved, trust me. Husam, they are here for me."

Husam was confused and asked, "Why would someone want to hurt you, Sister?"

"I wish I could have helped you earlier. Just lay low and make sure no one steps out of the classroom."

Nadia did his farewell. She knew she would not come back again. Hot winds were blowing. It was a scorching summer's day. As she stepped out, she could see at least five guys pointing guns straight at her. One of them screamed, "Show me your hands."

Nadia surrendered, raised her hands, and said, "Just don't hurt anyone."

The mercenary screamed, "This is not a negotiation!"

One of them moved toward her to capture her alive. Nadia had decided that she would not get caught alive. She was waiting for him to get close enough. As the mercenary approached her, he tried to tie her up from behind. There was silence all around the camp. Husam watched everything from the small opening in the curtained door, but he ensured that no one else watched the violating act. As the mercenary went behind

Nadia, she grabbed hold of him, snatched his weapon, and pointed the gun toward his head. She said, "I agree, it is not a negotiation."

The remaining lot aimed at her, finger on the trigger, but she was taking cover behind one of their guys.

Nadia knew it was time to end it once and for all. She remembered her childhood and parents, how she landed there, and all that she did in her past. She looked back at the school door and pulled the trigger, killing the ISIS personnel instantly, and as he fell onto the ground, the remaining merceries rained fire on her. They emptied their assault rifles on her, and Husam and the rest of the students screamed as Nadia fell to the ground. Husam witnessed the incident. He held his crutches and told the remaining students to remain calm and not come outside. They were all scared. They told Husam not to go as they feared that he might be killed. He went outside. He was already in tears, crying by the side of the dead body of his only savior in that camp. He fell to the ground and cried unbearably, holding Nadia's head on his thigh. One of the mercenaries commanded one of the men to remove the disabled boy away from her and instructed the others to get her belongings from her house.

As ISIS guys forcibly held Husam. He was not ready to let go of her, but what could he do? As he was grabbed and thrown away at a distance, the guy started recording the scene of action where Nadia's body was lying, and he said, "This is what we do to our enemies."

Once it was done, the other member of ISIS smashed Rukhsana's door and started throwing their stuff. Nafisa hugged Ruskhsana and sat in the corner crying. He asked, "Where is her stuff?"

Nafisa cried and pointed upstairs. They went upstairs, took away all her stuff, and went outside. Nafisa thought *we would never be safe as long as these monsters existed.* They were both unaware of Nadia's fate.

As the ISIS mercenaries left the Zaatari camp, they carried the dead body of one of their fallen soldiers. They informed Tariq about the successful execution of their mission, but still, a loss was incurred as the stubborn woman was not ready to surrender. Tariq inquired about her belongings, and one of them said, "We have all of it, Sir."

Tariq said, "Good job. His soul must have found a place in heaven. Come back."

Back in camp, the security guard was the happiest person. He said, "She was a spy, a traitor, and an enemy of the country. She deserved to die."

As soon as Nafisa and Rukhsana heard the news, they ran toward the school. They saw students encircled as they reached the school. Rukhsana broke down before she got to the school as she understood what had happened. She did not have the guts to face it. Nafisa also understood but prayed that her friend was safe. She saw Husam sitting on the ground, motionless, absolutely still, as if he had seen the devil. His eyes were not blinking. He was in shock. He did not understand what he just saw—was it a nightmare? Nafisa removed a few students and saw Nadia lying on the ground and blood spilling all over the place— everywhere. Nafisa broke down and started crying on the floor. She could not hold herself anymore. People began gathering gradually. They discussed that she was probably working for the Syrian government, so ISIS must have killed her.

Everyone had a different opinion about the event. They decided that she would be buried the next day, as it was almost evening. Her body was kept in the temporary school where she taught her students about hope and kindness. At present, she lay dead there. Nafisa, Rukhsana, and all of her students were present in the classroom. They prayed for her, except Husam, who was awkwardly quiet. The silence was not good for him, as he was not crying, and it was not expected. The incident left him with a deep wound in his heart. Nafisa knew it was not a good sign. All of them had only one question—*why her? What did she do that ISIS had to kill her publicly?* Husam had developed a feeling that whomsoever got close to him was taken away from him. All of them started leaving for their homes. Nafisa tried to console Husam, but he was not ready to let go of the fact that Nadia was no more. She wanted to take him to her house, but he was not going anywhere that night. Rukhsana suggested that he should be left there. Everyone left, but Husam did not leave the school that night. He did not sleep. He eventually cried and swear revenge against the ones who were responsible for her death. He remembered the first day Nadia arrived at the camp—almost a year ago. She brought peace and stability to him and many others as well. Everyone lost someone that day. For some, she was a sister, teacher, and friend. She was many things, but she worked with the government as per the rumor in the camp. Some opposed that idea entirely, and a handful of them believed in that theory. No matter what people thought, Husam lost his sister. Nafisa and Rukhsana lost a friend, and she was not coming back.

The following day, all her students gathered along with Nafisa and Rukhsana outside at a distance of a mile from the camp to give Nadia her last rites. She was buried alongside many others who lost their lives in the camping center. That piece of land had become a burial site for the people dying in the Zaatari camp. Everyone prayed for her. Husam came walking with crutches and carried a tombstone made up of steel, and Nadia's name was engraved on it. Everyone guessed who must have made it. Everyone started paying their tributes in the form of flowers, letters, and whatever they could find, which reminded them of her.

Slowly everyone started moving back toward the camp. Only Nafisa and Husam were left. Nafisa asked Husam, "What have you brought for her?"

He was quiet and said, "She took away everything which was hers. Now, I just have these books which are useless to me."

He kept the books near her grave and stood there silently. Nafisa brought a cigarette hidden inside some of her stuff, held it there and said, "You know something, it doesn't feel right—what has just happened. There must be a reason behind it. She used to say that she doesn't have much time left—as if she knew this was about to happen."

After thinking, Husam eagerly listened. He replied, "There is something out there that we don't know, but I will find out and I will not leave those who are responsible for all this."

Nafisa knew Husam needed support during such a tough time. He was close to her, and she did not want him to do something stupid and irrational.

Chapter 14

The Evil Game-plan

Tariq showed the video of Nadia's execution to Jacob and Amanda, who were as good as dead and knew that they would not leave that place alive. Tariq got hold of her stuff and found a satellite phone, some forged IDs, and a laptop. Tariq instructed his team to unlock that laptop as he wanted access to all the data. It was encrypted. His junior asked for some time. They wanted to open a secret service agent's device quickly—as they generally plan for every contingency. They eventually bypassed several security measures after working hard to decrypt the laptop. Still, they did not find anything significant except for three names—Husam, Nafisa, and Rukhsana, on the sheet where all their information was mentioned. Tariq thought that she was planning something around these people, but what? This was the question that was bothering him. He told his guys to try to connect with the camp guard, who helped them identify Rachel and learn more about what was happening in addition to those three people. After a few days of digging into the matter, the guard had something important to share. He told them that those people were leaving the camp for the United States under the Refugee program. The list was out on the desk in the UN office. As soon as Tariq was informed about that, he immediately hatched a plan to attack the US. Firstly, he instructed his mercenaries to disguise themselves as average Syrian refugees, and secondly, to rush to Husam and brief him about the plan. They left for Zaatari with a big project to change Husam's fate.

As soon as they reached the camp, they searched for Husam, as they had all the local intelligence from the guard who had become one of their field operatives and a worthy asset indeed. Husam never attended school the day Nadia died. Everything started becoming normal in the camp. There were new teachers, including Nafisa, who took over Nadia's place as she had already laid the foundation for it. Husam was not over the horrifying experience of that day and used to sit outside Nadia's house. He strained his vision in the hope of seeing Nadia once again.

His logical mind had accepted the event, but the emotional being deep inside was not ready to let go. Two men who looked just like some regular camp guys interpreted his daydreaming. One of them said, "My name is Imran. I heard you are looking for answers and revenge."

Husam asked confusingly, "What? Who are you?"

"It doesn't matter who we are. Are you willing to know the truth and identify the real enemy?" asked Imran.

Husam was a little angry and said, "I think you are looking for someone else. You got the wrong guy. Stop wasting my time and leave me alone."

Imran said, "You need to see this, Husam. You need to know that you have been fooled alongside many others in this camp and this country."

That statement grabbed his attention, and Husam said, "How do you know my name? Who are you?"

Imran said, "You need to come with us because we don't have much time."

The guard had arranged the room in the camp where the secret meeting was to take place. They all entered a small, empty house, which was completely isolated and the guard was securing the perimeter.

Husam was still not over what had happened a few days ago. Now, he was about to get enlightened on dirty geopolitical warfare. Imran opened his laptop, which contained all the necessary information to challenge any belief system of any particular community. Imran said, "What you are about to witness might seem disturbing to you, but it is the truth. You can't deny and doubt it."

He showed Husam pictures of Rachel in London. She looked like Nadia to Husam. Husam's confusion hit a new high. He asked, "Who is this woman? And why are you showing me her picture?"

Imran asked a counter-question, "You tell me who she is. Doesn't she look familiar to you?"

Husam looked at the pictures carefully once again. Yes, it was Nadia, but what was she doing in a foreign country? Husam asked himself such questions. He was shocked but controlled his emotions. He asked Imran, "Why does this woman look like Nadia?"

Imran said, "Because they are the same person, Husam."

Husam's heart started beating faster. He said, "I don't believe you. This can be a trick that you people are playing to deceive me."

Imran had instructions from Tariq to go slow and compassionately on the boy. Imran said, "You don't have to believe me. You must see it yourself, Husam."

Imran showed various pictures of Rachel Green in Ghouta as she was the one in charge of the operation. Husam almost had a panic attack. He was sweating but calmed himself down. He asked Imran, "Why?"

Why would she do all this, and why would she come here? Husam thought repeatedly. Imran said, "I know you have questions, but we don't have much time left. Listen carefully now. Her real name was Rachel Green, and she was a British spy. She did all this—she started this war. You don't have a leg and live miserable lives because of her and her people. She is **the one** who started this all—the only one responsible for everything. Don't be sad, Husam. She planned the Daraa Attack and later, the Ghouta chemical story. You must have seen it yourself. You have come a long way. There was never a chemical attack. False news had been spread all over the globe. She was one of them, following assignments and planning something big here in Zaatari. ISIS had to take charge of the situation and punish her for her past deeds. Husam, she had to die—she had to—for the numerous lives that she took."

Husam was in tears. He didn't know what to believe and what not to believe.

He still was not ready to believe whatever he heard and saw. *Why would Nadia do something of that sort, and why would she help young students to get educated and have a better life?* These questions were still bothering him. It was clear that she had a dual personality. It was undeniable, but Husam was hurt. In this scenario, he did not know who the main culprit or accused was in reality. Imran said, "Stop crying, Husam. God has plans for you."

Husam interrupted him and said, "I don't believe in God."

"But you believe in what you just saw. I have many shreds of evidence to substantiate my claims, Husam. This laptop is for you. It contains all the evidence of the events that she did and now you have a chance to redeem yourself from the slavery of the western world. Look around you—at what they did to gain control over our country. Thousands of Syrians have died, migrated, and gone missing due to someone's need for oil. From where do you think the rebels are getting arms and ammunition? CIA and Mi5, of course—from people like Rachel and others—who else?"

Husam was getting there where Tariq wanted him to be. Those speeches and findings were not eye-opening but mind-bending. Husam now had genuine questions about all that had happened—everything from Ghouta to Zaatari. He asked Imran, "If she is the one responsible, how did you manage to catch her?"

Imran replied, "She was a double agent, Husam. She served the British and sold vital pieces of information to other intelligence agencies. Her people were after her Husam, not just us. You need to have a broader approach to understand what is going on. All your answers are on this laptop."

Husam did not say anything, but the idea was planted in his head. His mind started asking questions that he had never thought about before.

Imran broke the silence and said, "We have made ultimate sacrifices and planned something for you, Husam."

"And what would that be?" asked Husam.

"We have put your name on the list of Syrian refugees who are leaving for the United States of America within a month. How about that?" asked Imran.

Husam said, "You mean to say I'm going to the US?"

"Yes, you are, Husam, and you don't know what a price we have paid to get your name on the list. I will leave it to you. Do you want solutions to the problems that our people have faced, or you are seeking solace for your fate? Are you seeking solace for your disguised teacher?"

The very idea that he would leave for the US made him feel relieved. Nadia used to say, *you will have a better life,* but after listening to Tariq, he thought otherwise. He asked Imran, "What do you want me to do?" All your questions will be answered once you explore the laptop's content, carefully review them and know what to do. Prepare yourself and never forget what she and people like her did to you and your people. I will leave now, but choose wisely and train yourself hard. Teach them a lesson, Husam, and make sure they also pay for what they did. God will be watching, and he has chosen you amongst all. Don't disappoint him. Syria will remember your sacrifice."

Imran left with his subordinates and told the guard that it was his responsibility to ensure that Husam was kept out of danger until he left the camp. Imran knew he had done his part. There was enough data to radicalize him and properly provoke his thoughts for the job. He informed Tariq that his work was half done. He was sure Husam would do the rest of it in time.

For the next few days, Husam only watched the hidden videos on his new computer. He stopped stepping out of his tent. He gave up football, which he loved for something more significant. He made sure that everything was kept a secret as it could prove fatal if somebody got a hand on it. For the first time, he heard and saw Abu Bakr al-Baghdadi, the leader of the Islamic State organization, which was first known as Al-Qaida before merging with the Syrian forces. His message was loud and clear—it was based upon the Holy Quran—to become soldiers of the Almighty. History shows that the people with a religious purpose in their lives conducted the most unholy acts in the world. When you have a God-given purpose in life, your thinking process becomes constrained to the drive itself and nothing else. Abu Bakr al-Baghdadi's speeches provided the necessary shelter for victims of the war to stand up again and fight to protect their religion. It was of utmost importance and held the highest spot in their lives. His words penetrated deep into people's minds and could be regarded as highly motivating. Husam started finding sense in what he was trying to convey. Once Husam knew that he was fooled from the very beginning by Nadia and her country, he decided to open the training module given by Tariq's right-hand man, Imran.

The module emphasized cyber-warfare. It would be hard for a boy who hardly knew how to use a cell phone to make him understand modern techniques. It was designed in such a way that gradually, he and many others like him would grasp it. The people who created and formed it knew there was no need to fight on the ground. This task required more analytical abilities than sheer physical strength. Husam was the perfect candidate. He fulfilled the criteria. Tariq's only gamble was regarding whether he would be able to deliver the results. He opened the folder, which contained information about Mi5 agent Rachel Green. He was still not over the fact that Rachel and Nadia were the same people. He missed her but at present, he was more interested in knowing more about her past. The files had adequate evidence to prove that Rachel was behind many Syrian attacks. However, it was not clear whether she was on a mission in the Zaatari camp. Husam saw her picture back in London. She looked the same. He asked himself, *why would she hide her past? Maybe she was guilty of her crimes and came there to help people for redemption.* Husam was convinced that she was not innocent, and he decided that he would not spare those who were directly or indirectly responsible for the condition that he and his citizens faced.

As Husam started exploring the new laptop, he slowly became engrossed. He used to sit in the corner of his room and watch those brainwashing videos. The videos radicalized his mind to a large extent. He knew his sole purpose in life was to serve his organization and start *Jihad*. In a few days, he knew what the internet was and how it worked, but not the *Dark Web*. They made him understand how the dark web can be an essential tool in destruction. It was tremendously complex, but once one knows its fundamentals, one gets the hang of it. The tricky part is understanding how to browse the dark web.

The question was finding and recruiting the right candidate for the job. This was the most challenging part of his job. He learned a few tricks on planting specific ideas into an individual, manipulating his thought process, and finally using them against the Americans. He was not fully ready to execute what Tariq had in mind, but he was slowly getting there.

The day arrived when the UN put up a list of people, who were allowed to leave for the US in their camp's office. Many people rejected those who had maximum expectations. On the contrary, the people with the most negligible chances of getting through had their names flashed in the open. Husam, Nafisa, and Rukhsana's names were there. Diana fulfilled the promise which was given to Rachel. Nafisa was thrilled that the UN recommended her name and was excited about the whole idea. She rushed home excitedly to inform Rukhsana. As she reached home, she hugged Rukhsana and started crying. Nafisa said, "We are going to the US."

The old lady did not understand and asked, "What? Where? How?"

Nafisa smiled and replied, "The UN office has put up a list. The Americans have allowed Syrians to migrate to the US under their new policy, and guess what? All three of our names are on the list. Can you believe that?"

Rukhsana was not as thrilled as Nafisa, but she asked, "Who is the third one? Nadia is gone."

Nafisa's smile on her face had gone when she heard the question. She forgot about Nadia completely. She said, "It is Husam. I know, and I'm sorry I completely forgot about her."

Rukhsana replied, "Good for you both. Listen, I'm grateful to them for showing such sympathies toward us, but I'm happy here. This is my home, and I will be buried here. I'm not leaving."

Nafisa was upset with Rukhsana's reply and the way she reacted. She said, "We need you, Rukhsana, please come with us."

Rukhsana asked, "We?"

Nafisa said, "Husam and I."

Rukhsana gave her a stern look and said, "Oh no! He needs you probably. You can take Nadia's place and console him. I'm not going to babysit him. Listen to me, no offense, but I'm done running from one place to another. This is my resting spot now. Tell the UN people to strike off my name and recommend someone else's name—one who wants to go abroad. I'm sure Moshin will come for me once the war is over."

She left the room after saying all that. She was upset and hurt and had seen enough of people dying around her. She decided to stay alone for the remaining days she had left. Nafisa was sad by now. She remembered the days when all three of them used to sit and have a good time together. Nadia's death had a severe impact on her. She thought of checking on Husam to see if he was also feeling the same way as her.

Nafisa went to check on Husam. As she was about to enter his tent, she saw him watching something on a laptop with earphones plugged into it. It was strange—how did he get a personal computer? As he did not hear the footsteps of someone arriving, he saw Nafisa right in front of him. He closed the laptop immediately and unplugged his headphone. His face became red like a thief who gets caught. Nafisa asked, "Where the hell did you get a laptop?"

Husam was scared. He had to come up with something fast. He said, "Oh, this? Somebody dumped it near the trash. Luckily, I found it, and it works fine."

Nafisa said, "You found it? Lucky you, I can't imagine owning things."

Husam tried to change the topic.

"You look sad. Why are you here?"

Nafisa was sad. She had assumed that Husam's reply would be the same as Rukhsana's. She said, "Listen, Husam, I know you are upset with Nadia's death. Trust me, I was also heartbroken. I lost my only friend. It is not like I don't miss her…"

Husam interpreted her in between and said, "You came here to tell me this?"

Nafisa's whole idea of the US thing was now slowly fading away. She said, "The UN's office has put up a list of names of fortunate people who may travel to America. You and I are some of the lucky ones. Listen, I know you don't like me much, but if you give me a chance, I will take care of you. Just come with me to the US. I don't want to lose this opportunity. Rukhsana has already said no. I don't want to go alone. I know I can't take Nadia's place, but trust me, I can be your friend, your sister—please, don't say no."

Husam only heard *the UN list*, and *his name was there*. Imran told him that he thought it was precise. They must have sacrificed many lives to put up his name. He felt God was with him and wanted him to perform that task for Syria and its people. He had a wicked smile on his face. Nafisa asked again, "You are smiling. Is it a *yes*?"

"Yes, I'm in. I have nothing left here. God has given me an opportunity, and I don't want to waste it. I'm coming with you."

Nafisa smiled and was contented now. She hugged him and started crying.

"Let us begin your life again."

Husam was only thinking of ways to destroy the US.

The day came when Husam and Nafisa finally managed to leave the camp and embark on a new journey to New York. They never thought that they would step out of that hell, but life had different plans. They both suffered a lot, like the others living in the camp.

They were lucky as they came in contact with Nadia or they would have gotten turned into rotting corpses like the thousand others. Nafisa was now a sister to Husam, and he needed her support as a family member in an obscure place.

Meanwhile, Tariq released a video on the internet in which Jacob and Amanda were executed separately by cutting their throats. Another clip was uploaded that showed Rachel's execution with a message from Tariq to the CIA and its allies, "This is what happens to spies and traitors. This is only the beginning—there will be more." Diana saw it and managed to remove it soon enough. The video did not find the target audience, that it was supposed to reach. Diana cursed Rachel for her decision to leave the Agency and lead a disguised life. Because of Rachel two of her agents died, and she died as well. Once Diana received the list of people she wanted on board, Rachel instructed Diana regarding what would happen once ISIS caught her. She told Diana to tell her parents that she had died in a plane crash. She made sure no information reached them about who she was, what she did, and how she died. Diana did what Rachel asked for before her death.

Chapter 15

Terms of Reality

(New York, 2017.)

Diana said, "I approved this list. She requested me to do this last favor for her. Now I understand it. They must have hacked her laptop and decoded all that they could get. They must have figured out that Husam was close to her, so they grabbed that opportunity and hatched this conspiracy."

Dan was still clueless but was starting to understand things a little bit. He said, "You mean one of your agents who first worked with you on a mission in Syria, helped Husam get here? But why?"

"She wanted him to have a good life in the US. Poor Rachel, she shouldn't have done it that way. ISIS got away with this. They had a better hand over us. They must have trained and brainwashed him so severely that he had no choice but to complete his mission."

Dan now had some idea of what was going on. This was nothing but a brand-new ISIS terror strategy to attack the world. Diana said, "Daniel, it is up to you now. You decide how you want us to end this."

"What do you mean? He is just a boy! We don't even know how much he has suffered, and you want to kill him?" said Daniel.

"I like the change in you, Daniel. I like how you think now."

Dan realized that she knew everything about him. "I didn't say we are here to execute him. Okay, I will give you a choice. You find out about his current mental state. You have seen war. You know how things are and how they work. Figure it out. Can you give me any guarantees that he won't do it again?"

Dan thought about it and said, "Yes, give me a chance to intervene, and I will tell you precisely what needs to be done. I can handle such a situation. These people are scared and harmless. I will take it, and please tell your force to back away."

Diana thought about what Dan had just proposed and said, "All right, Daniel. We will just move a step behind. I need to know completely that he is not a threat."

Dan said, "I'm on it, Ma'am. Just one more thing—it is out of context. What was that faculty in Dimona?"

Diana smiled and asked, "You tell me. You spent more than a month there. What do you think?"

Dan said, "It wasn't just a mere radar station."

"Then what was it?" Diana asked again.

Dan did not know what it was exactly, so he remained quiet. Diana spoke, "It was an advanced nuclear weapon research facility. I can't tell you more than this. Now do your job. We are awaiting your signal."

Dan got out of the car and moved toward his building. Everything was silent.

He wished that he had taken a similar kind of role back in Haditha. He called Nafisa from his flat and told her that he just needed to talk to Husam. He knocked on Husam's flat's door. Nafisa was already terrified, shivering and trembling with fear. She thought that maybe Husam had done something stupid that day. Nafisa asked, "Is everything okay? I'm terrified. We have brought the same situation from our past. Back in Syria, soldiers used to raid our homes. Tell me something, whom do you work for? Are you with the forces?"

Dan quickly calmed her down by saying, "Relax, no one will hurt you, Nafisa. I'm here to talk to Husam about something important."

"What did he do, Dan? Please tell them that he is not behind anything that happened today. How is he somehow involved in this?" asked Nafisa.

Daniel said, "He is not. It's just something related to his new job, that's all."

Nafisa was worried that he had not come to talk about their job in this situation of panic and chaos, but she was out of options. So, she eventually agreed and pointed toward Husam's room.

Dan moved toward the room. The door was open. Dan's only concern was that Husam did not commit suicide. As he opened the door, he saw Husam watching the sunset from his window. Dan was now at ease. Husam knew who it was and asked, "Are you here to arrest me, Mr. Ryan?"

Dan replied, "I'm not a police officer. I can't do that, and why do you feel you will be arrested?"

Husam did not say anything. Dan asked him again, "Would you like to talk to me?"

Husam replied, "What do you want to know, Mr. Ryan?"

"All of it. The truth, Husam," said Dan.

"All of it…hmm…I wanted to kill as many Americans as possible when I arrived, but after meeting you and seeing how you helped me get back to walking again, I tried to undo the things. However, it was too late, but I regret it now. Do your job and arrest me. I'm done here, and please don't let Nafisa know anything. She is way too emotional. She might not handle it well. I'm behind all this, and this is my last wish."

Dan said, "I told you earlier—I'm not here to arrest you. My question is *why?*"

Husam said, "After the Ghouta incident, my family was gone. I never saw my sister, Fatima, and my parents again. They probably died. I was transported to the Zaatari refugee camp, which was like a little city in the desert. The accident took away my legs. It made me crippled. I loved football, but I can only watch the game now and never play again. I tried ending my life many times but somehow, I couldn't. Then she came, just like you did here. She helped me learn a few things about history and spent time with me. I was happy and thanked God for giving my sister back to me, but God had other plans. One day ISIS militants attacked the camp. They searched—especially for her and finally snatched her from the classroom. They beat her, tortured her, and brutally killed her before my eyes. I cried the whole night, held her dead body, and swore revenge on those who did that to her. A week later, they came again, but they came for me this time. They trained me, and Imran showed me videos of her roaming the streets of Damascus. It was her. I swear it was her. They told me she was a British secret agent, and she was the one who planned the Syrian war, the Ghouta chemical attack, and the Darra attack. I wasn't fully convinced, but they showed me her real ID and left me with no choice but to believe them. After doing all this, I still had questions about why she came to a refugee camp. They told me that she came to the camp to spy on them. They gave me a God-given purpose to avenge those who killed us. They trained me in cyber warfare tactics and how to radicalize young Muslims, which I did. They put my name on the refugee list—to be transferred to the US. I wish you had come a little earlier, but I'm sorry for what I did. I just wanted to play football with my friends."

Husam broke down. Dan immediately consoled him and said, "Do you think ISIS was capable enough to put your name on the list? I know you have been through a lot, and I'm sorry for your loss. Even I lost a lot before reaching this place, and I know it's not easy for you. You need to trust me on this. Rachel made sure you landed in the US and not some terrorist organization. She wanted you and Nafisa to have a better life, Husam. These ISIS people just used you as a mere pawn to conduct such cowardly acts that they couldn't do and know they will never prevail."

Husam was still sobbing. He said, "Rachel? Her name was Nadia, not Rachel."

Dan thought, of course, she must have changed her name. Dan said, "Husam, Rachel, and Nadia are the same women. Yes, she was in the secret service and was involved in the Syrian war, but remember one thing. No matter what she was involved in during the Syrian war, no matter what she did in life, she made sure you had a better future. She put your name on that list—always remember this. Now I want you to tell me, how you did it."

Husam said, "I just use the dark web. It's a safe platform for all illegal activity. After months of searching and exploring the chat rooms, I finally found this guy who had shown interest in the videos that I uploaded…"

"What? Videos?" Dan interrupted Husam.

"I had these videos of our mentor, Abu Bakr al-Baghdadi in my hard disk and pen drive. It inspired me when they initiated me. It ignited a passion for Islam and its core belief. I used the same videos to inspire Umar, and he did what I told him to do," said Husam.

"Where is that data now?" asked Dan.

"Trust me, Mr. Ryan. I did try to postpone the attack, the day you told me that you would help me find a job at the football club, but it was too late. He would not stop. I destroyed the pen drives, but there was a backup in the hard disk."

Dan said, "You will have to hand over that drive to me, Husam, and nothing will happen to you."

Husam said, "I'm already dead, Mr. Ryan. I have nothing left to live for. Umar must have somehow redirected you and your police force here. I don't know. It's my fate if you kill me here. Maybe I deserve it. You can take the drive. It's right in that corner next to my computer table."

Dan grabbed the drive and quietly said, "I have the drive."

He was given a communication earpiece by Diana's crew in the FBI van and they were listening and recording the whole conversation. Dan was ready to cooperate with the agency on just one condition. If they figured out that Husam did it due to his history and nothing else, they might let him a chance to live. After listening to the entire conversation, Diana took the radio and said, "You did well, Daniel. Hand over the drive to me, and after an investigation, we might let him go. But first, hand it over to me."

Dan said, "Okay, I'm on it, and everyone step away from the building."

Diana ordered everyone to move back. Dan said, "It's okay, Husam. Nobody will hurt you. I'm here with you."

Husam just sat quietly. He didn't know what would happen next. Dan kept his hand on his shoulder and moved outside again, reassuring Nafisa that everything was okay. The force started moving out. Dan handed over the drive to Diana. She said, "Sit tight and watch him. You did well there. I can't assure you anything now, but, yeah, once the final report is there, I will leave him."

Dan agreed with Diana and said, "Yes, Ma'am. I will not let you down." They all left with security forces, and the people in Dan's building finally got out and opened the doors. Daniel, the executioner of many innocent lives, now stood as a savior for many.

After a month, Dan received a call from a private number. It was clear to Dan, who was there on the other end of the line. He picked up the phone to receive the call and said, "Ma'am, I was waiting for your call."

Diana says, "Meet me at Central Park at three o'clock."

"Roger Ma'am, I'm on my way."

Before he reached the park, he saw that Diana was sitting on a bench and feeding the pigeons. There were security guys on each corner. Dan moved toward the bar and said, "Ma'am."

"Sit down, Daniel."

Dan sat down quietly and watched the birds feasting peacefully. "I always thought our paths would cross each other again. You are not the same man I saw back in Dimona—troubled, anxious, worried, and living your life in guilt and shame. You have become sensitive to your surroundings and the people you live with now. Did you ever think you would become such a man who would try to protect the people you hated the most?"

Dan was listening to each sentence very keenly. He said, "All that I have become today is because of you, Ma'am Francis and Lieutenant Peter. Both of you helped me. I was a finished man back then. I owe my life to you both. My children are here because of you."

"No, Daniel. You are here because you didn't resist the change that life demanded from you. Eventually, you worked for life and not against it, and here you are, living an honorable life. I have seen people break down when the slightest things change. You can't fight against life. No one can."

Dan did not say anything. He was at peace within himself and his surroundings. Diana said, "The report suggests that the boy indeed endured a lot of pain and suffering, and somehow, we are responsible for this misery. He had been through a lot. Our intelligence suggests that he is not a threat to us anymore, but whatever he did can't be justified, ever. Think of the lives that were lost on Halloween— it's tragic. Sometimes, I don't know whose pain is deeper and whose joy is shallower. There are multiple reports of vehicular attacks all around the globe, and we all know who is behind them and how they executed their evil plans."

She hands Daniel two envelopes. He asks, "Ma'am, what's inside them?" "Have a look at them and see for yourself. Do let me know what you have decided. Good luck, Daniel."

Diana left, and Dan sat peacefully, watching the birds. He opened a letter in which Dan's name was mentioned. It was an offer letter to join the CIA. Dan was surprised—he did not see that coming at all. He had absolutely no expectations. He was not thrilled or overwhelmed, but he thought of it since he thought that he could help save some more lives. He opened the second envelope and it was meant for Husam. It was an offer letter from the New York Football Club. They had given Husam a job to participate in coaching management. Daniel was happy. Dan smiled, looked at the birds, and thanked God. It was almost Christmas, and the holiday season and festivities were about to begin. Dan went home and asked his daughters whether they would like to move to another locality. They felt at home and did not want to move out. But eventually, Dan rented a bigger flat in the same locality. Dan decided Nafisa would move in with him and asked his daughters if they liked her. They did not oppose the idea, which was a good sign. Dan paid a visit to Husam, who had given up all hopes in life. He was probably waiting for the security agency to grab a hold of him. Dan showed him the offer letter and said, "Hope is a good thing, Husam. You should keep it but don't confuse hope with expectation."

Husam became ecstatic when he had given up all hopes in life. He was shown an opportunity of a lifetime right at that moment. "Now go live your life to the fullest, without bringing up the past. Live the life that Nadia wanted you to live—always remember her."

Husam smiled after a long time. The smile which was hidden for years was brought back to his face again. He said, "I will never forget her, nor you, Mr. Ryan. You two are the rays of light in my life when darkness nearly consumed me. If it wasn't for you two, I would still be roaming in the Zaatari camp."

They both hugged each other. Dan said, "You have my number. I'm just a call away—anytime you need me. I'm always there for you. Take care, Mr. Coach. The one last thing that I will take away from you is your sister."

Husam understood the reference. He smiled and said, "She deserves you. You are a good man. I'm sure you will care for her."

Daniel said, "I will."

They went their separate ways. Husam shaved his beard got a new look and booked a cab and went toward the football stadium. There was only one thing on his mind—football, once again. He chose to become someone else rather than what Tariq, Imran, and ISIS wanted him to be. Dan took a train to DC to join the agency. Nafisa and his daughters started living together. This was precisely what Nafisa wanted from the beginning—*a family*. Dan called his father and told him that he would soon work for the government again and found someone special in his life once again. He should pay a visit to New York very soon—during Christmas.

www.ingramcontent.com/pod-product-compliance
Lightning Source LLC
Chambersburg PA
CBHW061341160726
47995CB00001B/118